Hiding in Pla
By Lucy Fel

Text Copyright 2017 ©

All Rights Reserved.

With the exception of quotes used in reviews, this book may not be reproduced or used in whole or in part by any means existing without written permission from the aforementioned author.

Warning: The unauthorised reproduction or distribution of this copyrighted work is illegal. No part of this book may be scanned, uploaded or distributed via the Internet or any other means, electronic or print, without the author's written permission.

This book is a work of fiction and any resemblance to persons, living or dead is purely coincidental. The characters are productions of the author's imagination and used fictitiously.

Cover Art by Posh Gosh.

Images from Pixabay.

Table of Contents

Blurb and Dedication
Chapter One
Chapter Two
Chapter Three
Chapter Four
Chapter Five
Chapter Six
Chapter Seven
Chapter Eight
Chapter Nine
Chapter Ten
Chapter Eleven
Chapter Twelve
Chapter Thirteen
Chapter Fourteen
Chapter Fifteen
Chapter Sixteen
Chapter Seventeen
Chapter Eighteen
Chapter Nineteen
Chapter Twenty
Chapter Twenty-One
Chapter Twenty-Two
Chapter Twenty-Three
Chapter Twenty-Four
About the Author
If You Enjoyed Hiding in Plain Sight

Blurb

Mallory Scott is an espionage operative, working for the British government. She's travelled all over the world, often going undercover and infiltrating criminal organisations in order to extract the intelligence needed to dismantle their operations and bring the perpetrators to justice. Given her usual targets are terrorists, people-traffickers, drug-traffickers and arms dealers, her latest assignment should be relatively simple. A small group of Brits is raking in serious money in the diamond-scamming business—and although their MO is theft and forgery, rather than hurting people, they still need to be stopped. But up until now, they've proved elusive—no one can catch them in the act, or find a shred of evidence against them.

That's where Mallory comes in. She follows the group to Amsterdam, planning to get her claws in to one of the gang. Luck is on her side, and within twenty-four hours she's lunching with Baxter Collinson, the youngest—and most handsome—diamond thief. What she's not expecting, however, is to get on with him quite so well. Attraction bubbles between them—and for once, on Mallory's part, it isn't an act. For the first time in her career, Mallory struggles with what she must do.

Can she ignore her heart for the sake of her career?

Dedication

To everyone reading this, thank you so much for picking up this book. I hope you enjoy it.

To my fellow Brit Babes, thank you for continuing to be a constant source of inspiration, support and fun.

Last, but not least, thank you to the Brit Babes Street Team for all your support and the giggles. You keep me going when things get tough.

Chapter One

Mallory Scott spotted the people she was looking for as soon as she walked into the hotel bar. Hell, she hadn't even needed to search; they were being so loud and obnoxious they were practically screaming for attention.

Stupid, in Mallory's opinion. If you were running an international diamond scam, surely you'd want to keep a low profile? But no, apparently these guys didn't give a shit. Not only were they screaming for attention—and getting it, she noticed, as other patrons of the bar shot them the occasional glare—they were also projecting the fact that they were filthy rich. They were supping on the most expensive champagne money could buy and demanding oysters and caviar be brought in. The overwhelming arrogance made her blood boil, but she consoled herself with the fact that by the time she was done with them, they'd be taken down by more than a peg or two—they'd be at rock bottom.

Heading for a table in a position where she could watch them, but remain partially hidden behind a pillar, she shook her head. She could hardly believe they'd kept their multi-million-pound enterprise going for so long. If they ran their operation as sloppily as their current behaviour indicated they might, it was a miracle indeed.

Not that it mattered. They could be running the tightest ship ever known to man, and she would still find a way to take them down. It was what she did. For years now, she'd been successfully infiltrating illegal operations of varying kinds, then gradually dismantling them from the inside. Before the criminals realised what was happening, it was too late—their wrists were practically in the handcuffs, their arses on their way to jail.

This project was different from the ones she usually handled. Her past takedowns included terrorist plots, kidnappings, drugs, people-trafficking… that kind of thing. She'd been involved because sending in police or military personnel wouldn't work. Not in those particular circumstances. To be truly effective, Mallory needed to infiltrate the organisations at the top, gain their trust—or at least enough trust to allow her to snoop—and acquire evidence of their involvement to ensure their convictions. Otherwise, rushing in and stopping the terrorists, saving people and so on, important as that was, would only affect a tiny part of the organisation. It was vital to dismantle the whole thing, from the big bosses and the money men, right down to the minions doing the leg work.

An added bonus to this approach was that the victims of these organisations, as well as being saved, would know that justice had been served to those that hurt them, and the knowledge that they'd never get the opportunity to do it again. It was dangerous but fulfilling work, and Mallory couldn't imagine doing anything else. She loved the adrenaline rush, the challenge.

And the challenge element was precisely why this job was different. In as much as it wasn't supposed to *be* particularly challenging. Intel gathered over the past year had pinpointed the what, the who—though they couldn't yet put faces to names—the where and the how, and that had been done covertly, without the need for an undercover operative. All that remained in this case was to find out the when, so they could be caught in the act. It should have been simple, really. But the group was careful, exceedingly so. One of their number was a hacker, meaning that trying to access their emails, internet search histories and voicemails, or tap their phones without being detected was almost impossible. They were smart.

Which meant the only option remaining was the old-fashioned approach.

A honey trap. It was Mallory's mission to attract the attention of one of the men in the group—hell, even one of the women if any of them swung that way—and slowly, slowly cultivate and exploit their relationship in order to get the information she needed. Then *boom,* another international criminal enterprise would bite the dust.

Which brought Mallory to her current position, dressed up in ludicrously expensive designer gear and half-hiding behind a pillar in the bar of Amsterdam's most exclusive hotel. Someone less experienced than Mallory might have found the idea of staying out of sight ridiculous. The aim was to get the *attention* of one of the gang members, after all. But Mallory was at the top of her game, the very best of the best, and she knew damn well that putting in a little groundwork early on would pay off in spades. Before she did anything, before she so much as batted an eyelash in the direction of the gang, she needed to identify her target. It was pointless trying to eye-fuck with a bloke from across the room, only to discover he preferred men, or was happily married and the faithful type. That would attract the wrong kind of attention. When she *did* get noticed by the group, she wanted it to be for the right reasons, and on her terms. If they caught even so much as a whiff of her deception, it would be game over.

So she would watch, and wait. Then as soon as she decided which one of the group was going to be her new boyfriend, she'd move in for the kill. Figuratively speaking, of course. Killing wasn't her job. She was capable of it, and over the course of her career had ended more than one life in self-defence, or in order to protect others, but she was no cold-blooded murderer.

She was something much more dangerous; something that no one ever saw coming.

Picking up the leather-bound cocktail menu, she used it to further obscure herself as she took in the rest of her surroundings. She'd already done a scan of the place in her peripheral vision as she'd made her way from the door to the table she now sat at, but before she fixed her attentions on her target, she wanted to make absolutely certain there were no other persons of interest in the vicinity. The last thing she wanted was to start eyeballing the group, only to discover they had some covert security bods in the bar, who were eyeballing *her*. She doubted it—their intel suggested that they only used hired goons when absolutely necessary—but it always paid to be cautious.

After a couple of minutes—luckily it wasn't a huge area, and therefore she didn't have to hold the menu in front of her face for too long, making her look suspicious or terribly indecisive—she was satisfied, and slowly lowered the cocktail list to the smoked glass table, then closed it with a slap.

As if by magic, a handsome waiter around her age materialised. "Hello, madam," he said in Dutch, a language that she was, luckily, fluent in. He'd have switched to English with no issues—the Dutch were well known for their excellent command of English, and in a place such as this, being multilingual would no doubt be in the job description—but she'd blend in more effectively if she spoke the native tongue. "What can I get you?"

She hadn't actually had time to read the menu, but it didn't matter. Cocktail selections were almost the same the world over, unless establishments decided to give drinks different names, or put a new spin on an old classic. Even if they did, though, she'd never been refused an old classic when she'd ordered one, whether it was on the list or not. "Hi," she replied, also in Dutch. "I'll take a Manhattan, please."

"Very good, madam. It'll be with you in a few moments."

"Thank you." She treated him to a wide smile, as well as exercising her best manners. It certainly couldn't hurt to establish a rapport with a member of staff. After all, there was a chance he might be useful at some point.

While she waited for her drink, she pondered her next move. The group was still there, still being loud and obnoxious, and had successfully managed to get their oysters and caviar. She rolled her eyes. That was one benefit to staying in such a high-end hotel, she supposed. There was serious money at stake, and the management would want to do anything possible to keep guests happy, knowing that word of mouth, particularly in circles with such funds at their disposal, was by far the biggest influence in bringing in more people. More people with money. And so it went on. Here, at least, money really did make the world go around.

She watched the group, careful not to seem as though she was staring. She wasn't yet ready to gain their attention. It was unlikely, she quickly realised. They were so absorbed in their own little bubble that she probably could have stripped naked and walked past their table and they wouldn't have noticed.

With happy guests and word of mouth on her mind, she came to the conclusion that, although the gang was happy, there were plenty of other people in the bar that weren't. The more champagne the group quaffed, the more their volume increased. And with that volume increase came plentiful sighs and glares from the bar's other patrons. But, in their bubble as they were, they didn't notice.

Mallory smirked as she watched one angry-looking man start to get up from his chair, only to be stopped by the woman he was with, with a hand on his arm and a shake of her head. Mallory didn't blame her. This hotel might be the most expensive and exclusive in the Netherlands, but it didn't mean drunken guests wouldn't turn nasty or even violent if confronted. Really, management should be getting involved at this point. Maybe she could hurry things along in that department and see if it helped her cause any.

Just then, the waiter returned with her drink. "One Manhattan, madam," he said, placing it on the table with a flourish.

"Great. Thank you." She deliberately glanced over at the group, then back at the waiter, her eyes wide and innocent. Quietly, she said, "I don't mean to make a fuss, but would it be possible for something to be done about those people? They're totally ruining the ambiance in here. *Not* what you'd expect from such an establishment."

The waiter—she peeked at his name badge; Erasmus—gave a tight smile. "It is already in hand, madam. We are working to rectify the situation with the absolute minimum of fuss. However, as an apology and gesture of our deep regret, your drink is free of charge. I hope it is to your satisfaction."

Keeping her eyes wide, she replied, "Oh, *thank you,* Erasmus. I hope it's okay to call you that. I really didn't mean to be a difficult customer, it's just…" she tailed off with a shrug.

Erasmus gave a quaint bow. "*You* are not the difficult customer, madam. You have been a pleasure. And of course it's okay to call me Erasmus. Please, if there is *anything* else you require, do not hesitate to let me know. I will be pleased to assist you." He smiled, then turned and walked away.

Admiring the view of his backside until it disappeared out of sight behind the bar, Mallory grinned. Unless she'd been completely mistaken, there'd been a glint in his eye, and emphasis on the *anything* part. When she'd figured he might come in useful at some point, she'd been thinking along the lines of maybe pumping him for information, or potentially using him to gain access to areas of the hotel she wasn't supposed to be in. But the more she thought about it, the more she leaned towards him being the perfect candidate for a little extra-curricular fun. Her target, whoever he turned out to be, was off-limits for the time being, at least. It sounded like he and his friends were about to be escorted from the bar, and given the amount of alcohol they'd consumed, they'd all be drunk for the next few hours at least, then hungover for several more hours after that.

Giving Mallory plenty of time to become more familiar with the layout of the hotel and its operations. Not to mention the members of staff.

One in particular.

Her grin grew wider.

Chapter Two

Mallory wasn't the slightest bit surprised when the knock came at her hotel room door. Although she'd been subtle, simply scrawling her room number on an old receipt she'd fished from her handbag and leaving it on the table in the bar, it had still been a blatant invitation. Particularly since her drink had been on the house, therefore giving no reason for it to be charged to her room.

She'd figured if Erasmus was smart enough to get the hint, then he deserved to get laid. If not, well then it was his loss, wasn't it? A man wasn't a necessity for her. If she felt the need to get off, then her right hand would serve the purpose perfectly well.

Moving from her position by the window, where she'd been standing admiring the view of the city, she headed for the door. She made sure her silky robe was in position as she walked. Just because she'd basically issued an invitation for him to visit her room for sex, didn't mean she wanted to look desperate, or as though she'd been waiting for him.

Peeping through the spy-hole—someone in her profession could never be too careful—she smiled when she saw her visitor was, in fact, the very one she'd been expecting. Keeping the smile on her face, she opened the door and immediately stood back to let him in. It wouldn't do for him to be seen loitering outside. She wanted to screw him, not get him into trouble for consorting with the guests.

Clearly getting her drift, Erasmus glanced up and down the corridor before stepping over the threshold into her room. Apparently he *was* smart, because he'd brought a bottle of champagne and two glasses with him, having the twin bonuses of being his excuse for his presence in her room if anyone *had* seen him, and also… well, champagne was just always a good idea.

"Hi," she said in his native language, closing the door behind him. "I'm glad you made it."

He was halfway across the room when he tossed his reply over his shoulder. "Hi. Yes, me too. It's been an… interesting day." Placing the bottle and glasses down on the coffee table, he then turned to face her, the sexual interest obvious on his face as he took in her appearance. "I was very glad to find your… invitation."

"And I'm pleased you accepted it."

"You…" His expression turned uncomfortable, much to

Mallory's confusion, and he fixed his attention on the plush carpet. "You will forgive me… it seems silly in the circumstances, but… I don't know your name."

Mallory clapped a hand over her mouth, hoping he'd see it as a gesture of surprise, rather than her covering up her amusement at her *faux pas.* She'd been so focused on the task at hand, spying on the gang she was here to infiltrate, that she hadn't been fully concentrating on her flirtation with the handsome waiter.

Hoping she'd rearranged her features into an appropriate expression, she removed her hand from her mouth and took a step towards him. "I'm so sorry, Erasmus. It completely slipped my mind. My name is Bea Winchester." The lie tripped off her tongue so easily that she was sure even a fellow intelligence officer would believe her. But as much as she disliked lying to Erasmus—he was, after all, nothing to do with her reason for being here; rather a pleasant diversion along the way—it was essential to maintain her cover. Plus, if curiosity got the better of him at any point, he'd easily be able to check the hotel's computer system and discover what name she had checked in under.

He closed the gap between them still further, and held out his hand. "It's very nice to meet you, Bea Winchester."

She took his hand, then was surprised when, instead of shaking, he gently twisted her wrist and bent to place a kiss on her knuckles. His lips were warm and dry, and her astonishment at his action swiftly gave way to arousal as he lingered there for a few moments, before releasing her.

"A-and you," she forced out, fighting to get a grip on her emotions. It wasn't at all like her to be so affected by someone, but in a bizarre twist of fate, the very fact that he'd surprised her, had surprised her. During her years in the service, she'd seen so many things, so many facets to human nature, that it was nigh on impossible to surprise, shock or faze her. She made a mental note to watch this man carefully. She hadn't got any vibes from him to indicate that he was anything other than an attractive barman and waiter, but it was entirely possible she wasn't the only intelligence officer watching the gang. Their activities were widespread, after all. Any number of countries could be keeping an eye on them, trying to bring them down. And not all of them would necessarily want to team up with the British in order to do so. The Brits had as many enemies as they did allies.

"So!" she said brightly, crossing over to the sofa, deliberately exaggerating the wiggle of her hips and bottom as she walked, hoping to distract him from her moment of being flustered. "It was *very* good of you to bring champagne. Shall we?"

Erasmus had followed her over to the seating area, and inclined his head, then reached for the bottle. With finesse born of frequent practice, or possibly he was an exceptional actor, he opened the bottle, snagged a glass and filled it, before handing it to her with a grin.

"Thank you." She smiled back, waiting until he'd poured his own drink before even thinking of taking a sip. There was a chance the bubbly could be poisoned, or drugged. It irritated her immensely that she had to even take such precautions, to consider that everyone she met could be out to get her, but it was an instinct that had saved her life on more than one occasion. Besides, it was ingrained so deeply within her that she'd never shake it. She'd probably still be looking over her shoulder when she was old and grey, and long-retired from the intelligence game.

Fortunately, Erasmus didn't seem to find anything odd in this behaviour. Instead, after filling his champagne flute, he took the seat opposite her, then leaned forward, holding out his glass. "To new friends," he said, tipping her a wink.

They carefully clinked the flutes, smiling at each other, before settling back into their respective seats. Mallory crossed her legs, then made a fuss of tugging the hem of her robe down. She was biding her time. As she fidgeted, she watched Erasmus in her peripheral vision, but saw nothing untoward. He was completely relaxed—or as relaxed as a man who'd come to a practical stranger's hotel room for sex could be, anyway—as he took a sip of his drink, and swallowed it.

Deciding that it was safe, she took a drink. She hummed with pleasure as the bubbles burst on her tongue and the flavour exploded over her taste buds. She swallowed, then smiled at Erasmus. "Mmm. This is very nice champagne, Erasmus. Nice choice. What is it?"

Leaning forward, she then reached for the bottle and twisted it on the table so the label faced her. She pursed her lips thoughtfully and nodded. It wasn't really her area, but it seemed to be a mid-range champagne, which was precisely what she'd expect from someone in Erasmus' salary range. He might work in an exclusive hotel, so his wage was probably higher than the equivalent job in a less expensive place, but he was hardly going to be rolling in cash. If he'd brought a top-of-the-range bottle with him, she'd have found it very suspicious. It would have indicated that either he wasn't who he said he was; that he'd stolen it; or that he'd charged it to her room.

Filing the information away in her mind, Mallory decided she'd scrutinised him enough. If he *was* there to harm her, he'd have made his move by now.

As she released the bottle and straightened, she looked up and caught his eye. Her heart skipped a beat at the expression on his face. It was blatantly obvious that the *last* thing on Erasmus' mind was hurting her.

He grinned widely, making his appreciation of her abundantly clear without being lecherous. And she could hardly chastise him, in any case. A glance told her that he'd been treated to an almighty fine view down the front of her robe as she'd bent to examine the bottle, and, despite all her tugging and fidgeting, the silky garment wasn't exactly designed to cover her modesty.

The arousal that had flickered into life at the unexpected gentlemanly kiss on the hand and had continued to smoulder ever since, now flared up powerfully. She returned his smile, appraising him right back, then proceeded to down the contents of her glass. It was still relatively early, so there was plenty of time to finish the bottle between what would hopefully be multiple sessions of sex. Neither of them had any illusions that he was here for anything else, therefore small talk was unnecessary. Beyond names, what more did they need to know? And, if she was being totally honest with herself, the names part was only a social nicety.

Wordlessly, she got up, still holding her glass. With her free hand, she collected the bottle and headed for the bedroom, knowing without a doubt that he would follow her. She entered the room and kept walking right up to the nightstand on one side of the bed, where she put down the glass and bottle. Then, mentally crossing her fingers, she opened the top drawer of the nightstand. She gave a mental fist pump as she spotted the array of condoms in there, though she'd have been more surprised at their absence. This was a top-of-the-range hotel in Amsterdam—they liked sex here. The city had a shop called the Condomerie, for heaven's sake!

Smirking, she reached in and grabbed a handful of the foil packages, placed them beside the champagne, then closed the drawer.

A light snort made her turn. Erasmus stood on the other side of the bed, and had also put down his glass. He shifted his gaze from the pile of condoms to her face, and raised his eyebrows. "You have high expectations, Bea."

She shrugged. "What's that saying? 'Shoot for the moon. Even if you miss, you'll land among the stars.'"

Chuckling, he walked around the bed. Stepping up close to her, he then paused, as if awaiting permission to proceed.

Mallory reached out and grasped his wrists, tugging him towards her to close the space between them. Looking up into his eyes, she murmured, "I'm sure you will not disappoint, Erasmus."

Pulling his wrists free from her grip, he slipped one hand around her waist, and the other into her long, blonde hair. He leaned his forehead against hers, and said, "I will do my very best to impress, beautiful Bea." Then he kissed her.

Allowing her desires to take over; and her brain, if not to switch off, to at least go into standby mode, Mallory relaxed into the embrace. If his kissing technique was anything to go by, then she was confident he would indeed impress. His lips moved sensually against hers, rapidly adding fuel to the flames of her arousal. A moment later, as his hand shifted from her back to her buttocks, hauling her up against his erection, his tongue sought entrance to her mouth. She opened up willingly, happily, tangling her tongue with his in an erotic dance that soon had them both breathing heavily and grasping roughly at each other.

Pulling away with a deep inhalation, filling her lungs with much-needed air, Mallory blinked.

Erasmus looked equally dazed, but seemed to recover more quickly than she. Gently releasing her, he shifted his hands to her waist and undid the sash fastening the sides of her gown together. Then, giving the material a little nudge, he grinned wickedly as it slid off her shoulders, down her arms and tumbled to the carpet. Taking in her lingerie, he raised an eyebrow. "Nice. But it'll be even nicer when it's off."

Chapter Three

Mallory folded her arms, enjoying the expression on Erasmus's face as the action pushed her ample breasts together and made her cleavage even more pronounced. "I'm sure it will. But," she pointedly raked her gaze up and down him, "there's just one problem. You're still fully dressed." She toyed with her bra straps, then slipped them off her shoulders.

"That can soon be rectified."

"Very good." In swift, efficient movements, she removed her bra and thong and dropped them to the carpet beside the bed. Then she sat on the edge of the mattress, swung her legs up and settled back against the headboard, out of his reach. "I'll be waiting right here."

"You drive a hard bargain."

"You have no idea," she shot back, smiling sweetly. Inside, she wasn't feeling even remotely patient. She was eager to see him naked, but wasn't about to let him know that. His ego seemed just fine without her boosting it. Emphasising her outward nonchalance, she leaned over to the nightstand and poured herself another glass of champagne. By the time she'd returned to the soft embrace of the pillows, he'd removed his shoes—which were lace-ups, slowing things down—his jacket, and his bow tie. So she hadn't missed too much, and fully intended to enjoy the rest of the show.

Sipping slowly at the bubbly, she watched Erasmus undress. He wasn't making it into a strip show—no *Magic Mike* impersonations here, sadly—but nor was he tearing off his clothes in his impatience to move things along.

Mallory admired his restraint. But even more than that, she admired the view. And bloody hell, was it a good one. Ever since laying eyes on him in the bar, she'd suspected he had a sexy physique hidden beneath that well-tailored suit. It hugged in all the right places, and his posture was great. Now, seeing it revealed, it was all she could do not to moan aloud.

Like her, he was blond, blue-eyed and pale-skinned. Not that it really mattered. She didn't have a type—an attractive man was an attractive man, no matter the colour of his hair, eyes, or skin. But he truly was a sight to behold. He'd unbuttoned his white shirt, revealing a delicious slice of his chest and abdomen, and showing off the dark blond hair that adorned it. Even as she silently begged him to remove the garment, she realised he couldn't; not yet.

Their eyes met, a cheeky twinkle in his as he stood there, fiddling to undo his cufflinks. Until they were gone, the shirt would have to stay. Fortunately, it didn't take him too long to take them off and carefully place them on the nightstand. While there, Erasmus surprised her again by scooping up the condoms and playfully tossing them at her.

She squealed indignantly, almost spilling champagne as she jerked on the mattress. "Hey! Any more of that and I might just change my mind, you know. I could call Security, have you thrown out…"

Smirking, he shrugged out of his shirt and let it drop to the floor. Christ, who needed Magic Mike and the gang when she had this guy? He didn't need music, or dancing, to get her motor revving. She wasn't going to start tucking money into his underwear, though.

Mallory took a hasty sip of champagne in an attempt to hide her lusty response. God, he was only half-naked, and already he was *incredibly* nice to look at. He was finely muscled; not too bulky, not too skinny, with pecs, abs and biceps she just wanted to *lick*. She could hardly wait to see the rest of him.

Pinning her in his gaze, which made her want to squirm, he asked, "Still planning to change your mind? Call Security?"

She gave a small smile and peered coyly at him over the rim of her glass. "Maybe I could be persuaded to give you a second chance…"

He hovered his hands in the region of his belt buckle. "You sure? Because I can just get dressed and leave, saving us both the embarrassment of me being escorted from your room."

Keeping her tone as light as possible, she replied, "No, no, I think I'm persuaded. It's all right, you can stay. Please, continue." She maintained the eye contact, but gestured towards where his hands were still poised to undo his belt.

"Well, all right. But only since you asked so nicely." His eyes were full of promise, full of exactly what he'd like to do to her, and Mallory felt so hot that she was in danger of scorching a hole in the bedding. And they'd barely even done anything yet. Clearly her right hand, though it did the job, wasn't quite enough—she needed to get laid more often. After all, there was nothing like a real live, sexy man who was capable of giving as good as he got.

Totally different, of course, to the men she slept with in the line of duty. It was a necessary evil. To gain trust, to maintain and build relationships, she often had to be someone's girlfriend. Or pretend to be their girlfriend, anyway. And the saving-myself-for-marriage bit rarely washed in this day and age, so sometimes, when the waiting, the excuses of not being ready started to wear thin, she had to, quite literally, lie back and think of England. It wasn't so bad. It was invariably for a good cause, and although she didn't enjoy it, she didn't feel tainted by it, either. For her, it was more like a business transaction. A wham, bam, thank you, ma'am, now spill all your secrets type thing. Though not so overt, obviously.

She likened sex for pleasure and sex for intelligence-gathering purposes to the difference between sitting down to a nice slap-up meal, and eating fast food at a motorway service station. One you would deeply enjoy, and take your time to savour every single delicious bite. The other you'd just shovel the food in as quickly as possible because it was calories and it stopped your stomach rumbling.

Erasmus was firmly in the slap-up meal category. And when he finally undid his belt, opened his fly and dropped his trousers to his ankles, he was upgraded to something even better: gourmet.

His tight black boxers did little to conceal his taut thighs, and the tantalising appendage between them. The outline of Erasmus's stiff cock was clearly visible beneath the material, and even from this distance, Mallory could tell she was going to be more than satisfied with this sexual encounter. His confident attitude and the minimal foreplay they'd engaged in so far told her that he knew what he was doing, knew how to please a woman. And his… attributes showed that he was physically up to the task, also.

She shot him a lascivious smile and raised an eyebrow, silently telling him she was waiting, but that she had no intention of begging. Instead, she bent her knees, tucking her thighs into her torso. If he peered at just the right place, from just the right angle, he would get a tiny glimpse, a hint, really, of her pussy.

He stood there, his thumbs hooked into the waistband of his underwear. As she moved, his gaze was inevitably drawn to the place between her legs, albeit mostly hidden, which ached for him. Ached so badly that he could probably see the moisture on her swollen folds and the insides of her thighs.

Whatever it was that he saw, it seemed to do the trick. Without tearing his gaze from her, he whipped his boxers down, causing his cock to slap against his belly as it flipped up from the confines of the material. Then he moved hurriedly towards the bed.

Mallory quickly put down her almost-empty champagne glass, sensing from the look on Erasmus's face and the length of his determined strides that whatever he had planned, it was not going to be gentle.

And that suited her just fine.

The mattress dipped as Erasmus's weight settled on to it, and he quickly closed the space between them. His pupils were dilated, and even if she hadn't been able to see his cock, she'd have still known how intense his need was. It was written all over his face.

She shifted so her head was on the pillows, then spread her legs as Erasmus straddled her and positioned himself between them. The movement was smooth, like they'd done this a thousand times before. Maybe between them, they had, just not with each other.

Smiling at the thought, Mallory enjoyed the sensation of Erasmus's warm body covering hers, and welcomed his lips as they pressed against hers once more. His cock drew sticky lines of pre-cum on her thighs as his tongue slipped into her mouth. She had to resist the temptation to raise her hips, to entice him inside. She wanted him there—Christ, did she, but not until he was wearing protection.

Wrapping her arms around his back, she drew him closer, then slipped her hands down to grip the backside she'd been so admiring. It felt even better than it looked—deliciously warm, and had just the right balance between hard and squeezable.

She couldn't resist; she dug her fingernails into his rounded flesh. He growled into her mouth and gave a sharp jerk of his hips, bringing his cock that bit closer to her pussy. She moaned, then deepened their kiss. Before long their lips, teeth and tongues clashed together frenziedly as they fought for dominance, and their hands busily grabbed, gripped, squeezed and clawed at each other's bodies. All the while their grunts and moans rang out into the room, each one bringing them closer to the tipping point, the point where one of them would give in and reach for the nearest condom.

Despite the damp patch beneath her bottom, caused by her intense arousal, Mallory was determined she would not be the one to break. She was fucking Erasmus because she wanted to. It was nothing to do with work, so why rush it? They had all night. He was gourmet, not fast food, and she most definitely intended to savour him. And hopefully she would be treated to more than one course.

With that in mind, she put her hand on his chest and gently pushed him away. He looked dazed for a moment as his eyes refocused, then shot her a questioning glance. She patted the bed beside her. "Lie on your back."

After giving her a quick kiss, he did as she commanded, but not before, she noticed, snagging a condom and hiding it in his hand.

She pretended not to notice. It didn't matter. Even if she hadn't seen him do that, the thing she had planned for him next would guarantee he caved in first. Luckily for Erasmus, extracting intelligence wasn't the only thing she was good at.

Shifting onto all fours, she then manoeuvred so she was in between his legs. Putting her weight on her elbows meant her hands were free. It had the added bonus of thrusting her backside high into the air, which afforded Erasmus a damn good view. He'd be able to see her sucking his cock, her breasts hanging heavily beneath her, and her curvy arse, too. A real visual feast which she was sure he would enjoy.

Wrapping her fingers with deliberate slowness around his shaft, she let out a low moan at the sensation. Soft skin covered rigid flesh, and the fierce heat radiating into her digits was sublime. Lowering her head, she let out another moan as the scent of raw maleness hit her nostrils—musky, salty, and sexy. She couldn't wait any longer. She licked her lips, then parted them and sunk them onto him.

A strangled yelp reached Mallory's ears, and since her mouth was otherwise occupied, she smiled to herself as she lowered her head yet further. Erasmus's lovely cock slid over her tongue, its girth stretching her lips wide and soon after, flirted with her gag reflex. She pulled back and began to tease him with her tongue, using it to hug his shaft, then flick it in unpredictable patterns over his heated skin.

Now his dick was nice and wet, she created suction around it and began bobbing up and down, sucking hard while allowing plenty of saliva to dribble from her mouth. The rude, slick sounds rang out, mingling with the increased volume and frequency of Erasmus's moans, gasps and expletives. His thighs were tense beneath her palms, and his free hand was fisted tightly into the bedclothes.

She was clearly hitting the spot. The only question was: did she want him to come in her mouth, or should she make him wait a little longer?

Chapter Four

  The following morning, Mallory woke up feeling sore in all the right places. Memories came flooding back into her consciousness, and she smiled. Utterly satiated, she stretched, then gasped as her fingertips brushed against something warm. Some*one*, actually.
  She turned her head, and her mouth dropped open as she took in the sight of Erasmus beside her. His hair was mussed, and he'd pushed the duvet down a little, giving her a delightful glimpse of his broad shoulders, biceps and pecs. After a moment of watching him sleep, his sensual lips slightly parted, she tore her gaze away and tried to calm her racing heart. It wasn't that she was displeased he was still there as such, more that she was utterly dumbfounded. She'd never had a one-night encounter before where she'd woken up in the same bed as her lover—whether she was the one disappearing in the night, or he was. It simply hadn't occurred to her that Erasmus would stay, therefore it also hadn't occurred to her to bring up the topic.
  Now she had to figure out how to get rid of him in the nicest way possible. She didn't want to offend or piss him off—she'd be sticking around for a while, so she didn't want any awkwardness, and there was still a chance he'd come in useful at some point. She might even invite him into her bed again, if her work gave her further opportunity for some downtime. He was definitely worth a second go around… or more. She rolled over and grabbed her phone from the nightstand so she could see what time it was. 7am. Knowing her targets wouldn't be up and about for a while yet, she decided to get a couple more hours' rest. Erasmus was fine where he was, for now.
  When she woke again, it was 9:15. Still plenty early enough for her to do what she needed to do that day, but as a hotel worker, it could be a completely different story for Erasmus.
  Work. That was the key. Nodding to herself, she turned to face Erasmus. She laid her hand on his bare shoulder and gently shook him. "Hey, Erasmus. Wake up. It's after nine, do you have work today?"
  She wasn't entirely sure what she would do if he said no, and stayed snuggled up in her bed. She supposed she'd have to tell him her cover story—say *she* had work to do and kick him out, nicely, so

she could get on with her own day. But she preferred not to give any reason at all. The less she told people about her, even if it was complete fabrication, the better.

"Hmm?" He rolled onto his side, facing her, but didn't open his eyes.

Mallory shook him again, a bit harder this time. "Hey, wake up. It's after nine!"

"Huh?" That seemed to compute. He opened his eyes, which were still dull with sleep, and frowned. "What time?"

Patiently, she repeated herself. "9:15. I didn't know if you had work today, so I thought I'd better wake you, just in case."

"Shit! I'm glad you did, I have to start work at 11." Pulling himself up in the bed, he then leaned over and gave her a quick kiss. "I've got to go, I'm sorry."

"Okay, no problem." She put on a tone that she hoped portrayed mild disappointment and understanding all in one, while inside she heaved a huge sigh of relief.

Erasmus had got out of the bed and was hurriedly pulling on his clothes. Not wanting to seem uncaring, she reluctantly slipped out of the warm embrace of the duvet and grabbed her robe, ready to see him to the door and say goodbye.

His cufflinks were still on her nightstand, so she scooped them up and handed them to him. "Thank you," he said, taking them with a smile. He seemed more awake now. "I'm on a double shift today, unfortunately, but perhaps you'll pop into the bar later?"

She returned his smile. "I'll do my best, but I can't promise anything."

He nodded. "All right. Well then… I'll see you around?"

"Of course. I'll let you out." They walked out of the bedroom and to the main door together, and Mallory opened it.

Erasmus peered out into the corridor before stepping over the threshold. There was no one around, so he turned and leaned back in through the gap to give Mallory a kiss. Just then, she heard the click of a door opening nearby. It was so close it could only be the next door or the one opposite that. Figuring that whoever it was would look away from their public display of affection, therefore hopefully not realising Erasmus was a member of staff, she slipped her hand around the back of his neck and deepened their kiss. Continuing just long enough to give the other guest time to walk down the corridor away from them, she then released Erasmus.

Grinning, he ran a hand through his hair, making it even messier. "Wow. That was a nice way to start the morning."

"I couldn't agree more. Now shoo." She wafted her hands playfully. "I don't want to be responsible for you getting into trouble at work."

Nodding, he spun on his heel and headed in the direction of the lift. He soon caught up with the person she'd heard leave their room, whom she now saw was a man. As Erasmus drew level with, then passed the other man, they exchanged a greeting. They were far enough away by now that she couldn't hear what they said, but assumed it was "good morning" or something along those lines.

What she didn't expect, however, as she leaned lazily against the doorframe, watching, was for the other man to turn around. He'd clearly gotten a good look at Erasmus by now, identified him as a member of staff, and wanted to see where he'd come from.

She froze in position, knowing that ducking hurriedly into her room would just draw more attention to herself and what she'd been up to. The man took in her appearance; her no doubt extreme case of bed head, the bare legs and feet beneath the silky robe, and flashed her a smile so wicked she was sure it had been forged in the very bowels of hell, by the devil himself.

It was only then, as she forced herself to maintain eye contact and as a result got a good look at him, that she realised who he was. He was only one of the bloody gang she was here to infiltrate and take down!

He looked different this morning, in jeans and a sweater, rather than the expensive suit he'd been wearing the previous day. But it was undoubtedly him, the youngest male member of the group, and the one she'd earmarked as the one she would be most likely to be able to get her claws into.

Mallory wanted to kick herself. She'd wanted to get his attention all right, and in such a way that it didn't look deliberate on her part, but not like this. It was imperative that he saw her as desirable, as getting into his trousers was the goal, after all. But now there was more chance that he saw her as someone that frequented luxury hotels and made a habit of having one-night stands with the staff. Someone... well, *easy*. That had not been the plan *at all*.

She was just wondering how the hell she could rectify her colossal mistake when her diamond man did something else she hadn't expected. He tipped her an outrageous wink, then wiggled his eyebrows, before recommencing his journey to the lift. Erasmus had already called it, and it arrived just as her target got there. Both men stepped in together. As one, they turned to face her, both grinning, both wearing utterly lascivious, shit-eating expressions.

Confident that from this distance it was impossible for them to know exactly who she was looking at, she eyed the diamond man, smiling and giving a flirty little wave as the doors slid shut.

Only when they'd disappeared from sight, and the metal car was transporting both men to their respective destinations did she let out the breath she'd been holding and sag against the doorframe. Holy fuck! That had been… nerve-wracking. Years in her job, and therefore years of practice, meant she was good in situations like this, good at hiding her true emotions, but that had been bloody close.

However, it seemed that all was not lost. Her target had seemed incredibly amused by her grin and flirty wave. Possibly because he knew damn well she'd spent the night in bed with the man standing beside him, who thought her gestures were aimed at him, and him alone.

So, apparently, he didn't care that she was the sort of person who screwed hotel staff. That was a definite bonus, one she could hopefully use to her advantage. And now, the two of them had a secret. He knew what had happened. He also knew that she knew that he knew.

Heading back into her room, Mallory thought hard. She had to figure out how she could meet the guy properly, without it looking as though she'd orchestrated the meeting. As far as possible, everything that happened between them had to come from his side, or at least appear to. That was the best way to minimise the risk of any suspicion falling on her throughout the mission. If he started to wonder about her, about her motivations, then the game would be up. And it wasn't a game. Although their enterprise wasn't as dangerous as others she'd infiltrated—in as much as they weren't distributing arms, drugs or people—she had no doubt that if her cover was blown, her life would be in danger.

Criminals—no matter their particular brand of crime—were generally very fond of the benefits of their trade, so if they had to fight for them, they would. And in this case scenario, there was a hell of a lot of money involved. So if they discovered who she was and what she was up to, they would want to hurt her. *Bad.*

She walked over to the coffeemaker and switched it on, still wracking her brain as she waited for the gadget to do its job. The caffeine boost that was coming her way would surely help the thought process.

There had to be a way she could turn recent events to her advantage. Drumming her fingertips on the counter in front of her, she tried to put herself in the diamond man's—God, she had to think of a better nickname for him—shoes. What had *he* been thinking when he'd seen her kissing one of the hotel's members of staff? What went through his mind when he realised they'd spent the night together? She'd already surmised he didn't have a negative opinion of her. He'd been amused, not disgusted by, her actions.

It wasn't until she'd downed half the mug of coffee that a plan started to develop. Bloody hell—she'd been overcomplicating things. Diamond Man had witnessed Erasmus leaving her room, and hadn't seen anything wrong in her behaviour. But what did he think of *Erasmus's* conduct? There were rules, even if they were unwritten, about fraternising with guests, and if his superiors found out…

That was her angle. Somehow, she knew that there was no way Diamond Man was going to rat Erasmus out to his employers. He'd found the whole episode entertaining. Besides, it was none of his business, and he had absolutely nothing to gain by interfering. But *he* didn't know that she knew that.

So, instead of lurking in his orbit and hoping he approached her, she'd wait until he was back in his room, or until she saw him somewhere in the hotel by himself, and she'd throw herself on his mercy. She'd beg him to keep quiet about what he'd seen, lay it on thick, and see how things went from there.

It was going against the grain of everything having to come from his end to avoid suspicion, but it was a valid enough method to ensure she appeared genuine.

And if it didn't work… well, she'd just have to think of something else, wouldn't she?

Chapter Five

Ninety minutes later, Mallory hit the streets. She'd used the time she'd spent getting ready wisely, formulating a plan, thinking through different possibilities and outcomes, and therefore giving herself the best chance of success.

In her experience, all the intelligence in the world didn't compare to actually being on the ground and seeing where her targets operated. But she wasn't going to just wander in to Coster Diamonds, the premier diamond hotspot in the city, empty-handed. It was just up the street from the hotel, which also happened to be near to lots of designer shops. Dior, Chanel and Louis Vuitton were just a few of the businesses that had premises in the area. She planned to frequent some of them, do some shopping, then head on to Coster Diamonds and its adjacent museum laden down with carrier bags. That way, she'd come across as a typical shopper, one with money, and therefore not appear out of place, or look like a tourist just there to stare at the shiny things with no intention of buying.

She had no doubt that this tactic would attract plenty of attention from the diamond salespeople, but it wasn't really a problem. If they were chatty, it would give her the opportunity to learn more about the industry in general, and who knew, she might even be able to steer any conversations she had in a direction that would more directly aid her efforts. If she got *really* lucky, she'd spot one of the gang in the area. Either way, she had nothing to lose.

With a dubious glance up at the leaden sky, she reached into her handbag to make sure she had an umbrella. She did. Settling it towards the top of the bag for easy access should she need it, she then set off down the street, pleased to note she turned a few heads as she did so—both male and female. Once again, she was dressed in ludicrously expensive designer gear, which would help her fit in when she entered the shops, and had put considerable effort into styling her hair and applying her makeup. She looked good, sexy but classy, and she knew it. In her profession, attracting attention was usually the exact *opposite* of what she tried to do. But on this occasion, it was an essential part of the mission.

Her spiked heels tip-tapped on the pavement as she made her way from the hotel to the shopping area, careful to avoid run-ins with the ever-present, ever-in-charge cyclists.

She made it to Pieter Cornelisz Hooftstraat without incident, and made a beeline for the first shop of interest she spotted. Within moments she had the undivided attention of a personal shopper, and had decided to purchase a couple of small items. Her choice was nothing to do with cost—her bill was being footed by her employers, in any case—but to make sure the bags she ended up with weren't too bulky or too heavy. It was just common sense. If she bought, for example, a three-piece suit, the establishment would insist on having it sent on to her hotel, leaving her without a carrier bag to show for her efforts. No, it was very important that by the time she arrived at her real target establishment that she looked as though she'd had a busy day splashing the cash.

One clutch bag, a pair of earrings, some sunglasses and a scarf later, and she was halfway down the street. Then she noticed the lingerie store. Unable to resist, she headed in, her attention immediately caught by a gorgeous black lace basque. Fittingly, it was studded with tiny diamonds. Highly unlikely they were real ones—even at that price—but the effect was still stunning. She walked over to the rail and located one in her size, as well as the same design in a traffic-stopping red, then made for the changing rooms.

She tried both garments on, despite the fact that, hue aside, they were identical. She liked to see how the colours looked against her skin. She had already been confident that the black would be striking against her pale skin. But red often ran the risk of washing her out. On this occasion, though, it wasn't the case. Teamed with a closely-matched lipstick, it would look just as good as the black.

Two basques it was, then. On her way to the till, she selected two pairs of hold-ups which would go with the lingerie. The woman behind the counter smiled and simpered, and tried to persuade Mallory to add a bottle of their latest fragrance to her purchases. Conceding that the scent was, in fact, divine, Mallory agreed. But that was it—no more. She had enough designer-store carrier bags now to fit in, to look like a serious player, someone who could actually afford diamonds. She wondered if she'd get away with buying some. Maybe just a teeny, tiny pair of earrings? The platinum card she carried, emblazoned with her cover alias, would certainly allow the transaction to go through, but she doubted HQ would be so accommodating when they found out what she'd done. That might be taking it one step too far.

Smiling and thanking the shop assistant, Mallory picked up

her purchases and left the store. Her destination was actually more or less on the same street as her hotel, but she went a different route, not wanting to walk past the hotel again before getting there. Should anyone be paying her any attention, they'd surely think it odd if she didn't drop off her purchases before heading onto Coster Diamonds. And of course, dropping them off would be defeating the object of buying them in the first place.

The sky had grown even darker during her time in the lingerie store, and she mentally crossed her fingers that the rain that threatened wouldn't materialise. Holding her umbrella now, with her hands as full as they were, would be somewhat of a challenge.

Fortunately, it wasn't an issue. She reached Coster Diamonds, or *Royal* Coster Diamonds, to give it its full name, without a droplet of rain having fallen. The place was world famous, she learned, often used to make and clean jewellery for royals, heads of state, celebrities and generally folk with a shit-ton of cash.

Amsterdam had been a diamond centre since the sixteenth century, and Coster seemed to be the uppermost business, so it was no wonder it was a beacon for the criminals. An enticing lure. They were already taking insane risks, so why the hell would they bother to go small? They wouldn't. She'd seen firsthand just how arrogant they were. They were bound to go for the biggest fish in the pond. And this was it. The mother lode.

She painted a politely interested expression on her face as she explored the building, figuring out precisely what it held, and what it might be hiding in the parts which were off-limits to the public. The entire time, she was fully aware of the people around her, the salespeople, the diamond experts, the tourists, and others like her. Or at least, like the woman she was *pretending* to be.

A couple of displays in particular amused her. One was all about how to tell the difference between real and fake diamonds, and the other was about famous diamond robberies. She knew that the group she was looking to bring down had their fingers in both of those particular pies, and they probably found the display boards pretty hilarious, too. So far, though, she hadn't spotted anyone she recognised from the previous day, or anyone else of interest. For now, at least, the place was exactly as it seemed.

Keeping her cool demeanour became considerably more difficult when she hit the shop. This was no ordinary gift shop. It was packed with diamond-encrusted watches, rings, necklaces, bracelets, earrings, cufflinks… If you could put diamonds on it, they sold it. There were no prices on anything, which was never a good sign. But she had to rein it in—the whole point of her cover was that she could afford any of this stuff, *if* she wanted to buy it. She decided not to sail too close to the wind with her boss's favour, though, and wandered through the area, flicking looks of mild interest at various items, but behaving for all the world as though she'd seen better—*owned* better. The Shania Twain song, *That Don't Impress Me Much* floated into her mind, and she allowed herself a wide grin as she made for the exit.

As she stepped out onto the pavement—the sky, mercifully, had lightened—she spotted something very interesting. Standing next to the metal railings surrounding the building's small garden, mobile phone clutched to his ear and muttering fiercely into it, was her target. He didn't appear to have seen her. She shifted marginally back towards the door so she was less noticeable, and pulled out her own phone. Flipping it on to silent mode, she acted like she was speaking on it. Or listening, at any rate. If he glanced in her direction now, he'd recognise her, of course, but it wouldn't look like she was watching him.

Swinging her bags of purchases casually and nodding, uttering the odd "Mmm-hmm", "yeah" and "absolutely" into the phone, she actually spent the time having a damn good spy on her target. He was far enough away that she couldn't eavesdrop on his conversation, but she managed to glean that he was speaking English, and that the conversation was actually more of an argument. Or that the two people talking were stressed out about something, anyway.

Somehow, she had to turn this to her advantage. She already had, in a way. The fact he was even here, outside this particular establishment, confirmed the intel already collected. Her target and his buddies planned to steal one of the most famous pieces from Royal Coster Diamonds and replace it with a forgery. All they needed to know was exactly when.

Glancing over, she saw he was calming down. His tone of voice was more normal now, and his body language was relaxing. Hopefully that also meant that his telephone conversation was drawing to an end. She "ended" her own conversation, spent much longer than necessary returning her phone to its place in her handbag, and hoped that he'd soon be on the move.

Once again, luck was on her side. He was heading in her direction, and although no longer on the telephone, seemed lost in thought. Looking down, she began ferreting in her handbag for nothing whatsoever, while moving out into the pavement at a snail's pace, aiming to wander right out in front of him and orchestrate a "meeting."

In her peripheral vision, she could see that they were seconds from collision, unless he pre-empted what would happen and moved. But she'd make sure, somehow, that she got right in his way.

She was so focused on her objective, that she didn't sense the person close behind her until it was too late. Nimble fingers slipped into the handles of a shopping bag she held in her left hand and snatched it from her. She spun on her heel, watching open-mouthed as the young man ran off with his prize, the designer label on the bag taunting her as it bobbed away.

Shit, shit, bollocks and bugger—the bastard had gotten her sunglasses! On the positive side, he'd only gone for the bag furthest away from her body, rather than aiming for the whole lot in that hand, but still. Heart pounding, she yelled, "Hey, you bastard! Stop, thief! Stop that man!"

Normally, in her more usual attire of jeans and trainers, she'd give chase. What's more, she'd catch him, take him down, get the goods back and perform a citizen's arrest. But she couldn't run in these shoes or clothes, and doing so would completely obliterate her cover of rich, classy lady. No, she'd just have to shout a lot and appear distressed, then call the police.

But then, in a spectacular stroke of irony, her target, having seen what happened, called to her, "Wait there, and call the police! I'll get the bastard for you."

Turning tail, he sprinted after the thief, leaving Mallory standing slack-jawed on the pavement, trying to work out whether this would turn out to be a good thing or a bad thing.

Chapter Six

Heat suffused Mallory's cheeks and her heart lurched as she realised not only had she well and truly snagged her target's attention, but that of everyone in the vicinity, too. Concerned faces were turned in her direction, and, much to her horror, so were a couple of smart phones—probably filming. Or at the very least, taking photographs. *Fuck.* Her blood ran cold. That was bad news indeed, and something she would have to notify HQ about, to see if they could make the videos and photos "disappear" somehow. Technology wasn't Mallory's forte, but she had complete faith in the team back in London—they could perform miracles, and regularly did. To do her job safely and effectively, she had to be a ghost—so no social media accounts, no online presence, no way of identifying her or having evidence of her being in a certain place at a certain time.

A woman around Mallory's age approached her. "Hello," she said, her Dutch accent heavy, but her English excellent, "are you all right? Did he hurt you? Would you like me to telephone the police?"

Her stunned demeanour not a complete fallacy—she wasn't used to being gotten the better of—Mallory blinked, then shook her head slowly. "I'm fine, thank you. No, he didn't hurt me. And thank you for the offer, but it's all right, I'll phone them myself now. I'm just a bit shocked, you know? I can't believe the audacity of some people, stealing like that in broad daylight in front of so many witnesses."

The woman shrugged. "Unfortunately, it happens. Especially in cities. Are you sure you're okay?"

Mallory nodded, and offered a smile. "Yes. Honestly, I'm fine. Thank you, though, you're very kind."

"You're welcome. I hope that man gets your belongings back for you." The woman returned the smile, then slowly stepped back before turning and walking away.

Mallory once again retrieved her phone from her bag. As she dialled the number and put the handset to her ear, her stomach flip-flopped. What the hell were they going to say?

The line was picked up almost immediately, and Mallory recognised the voice of one of the support team, Simon. As luck would have it, he was also one of the technology experts.

"Hello," she said, looking around to see if her target was

returning, whether it be victoriously or not. "Do you speak English?" She paused long enough to give time for a response to anyone that may be listening at her end. "Oh, good. I need to report a theft. I am outside Royal Coster Diamonds in the city centre, and a man just snatched one of my shopping bags and ran away. Someone has chased after him, but I can't see them. I don't know where they've gone, or what's happening. A lot of people are around, and I think some of them may have filmed what happened on their smart phones, or maybe taken photos, so they may have the man's face on camera."

"*Shit,*" came Simon's response down the line. A moment passed—he was clearly figuring out the best course of action. "All right, Spider," he used her codename, as was procedure, "I understand what you're saying and we'll get right onto it. So you're outside Royal Coster Diamonds. The main entrance?"

"Yes. I just stepped out of the front door, ready to head back to my hotel, when it happened." She glanced up and around. "I can't seem to see any sss—CCTV cameras." She'd stopped herself just before she'd said surveillance, rather than CCTV. A civilian would be unlikely to use the word surveillance.

"Noted. I'll get one of the others to double check that. Much more urgent is finding and… disposing of… any close-up footage or images there might be of you, Spider. Don't worry, though, we'll get it done." He sighed. "Smart phones may have their uses, but they're also a pain in the arse. This happens more often than you'd think."

"Okay, thank you very much. I'll just wait here, then, until the man who gave chase returns. To say thank you. I should speak to him, *for sure.*" She mentally crossed her fingers that Simon would pick up on the hidden meaning of the words she'd emphasised. There was no way she could spell it out more explicitly without giving the game away.

There was a brief silence, then Simon said, "Spider, are you telling me that the man who's chasing after your thief is your target?"

"Yes, that's right."

"Bloody hell, you don't do things by halves, do you? Do you need me to send out a police officer, to help maintain your cover?"

"No, thank you, I don't think that will be necessary." Again, she looked in the direction the two men had gone. This time, she saw her target returning. He was by himself, and he clutched her shopping bag and wore a triumphant expression on his handsome face. "The man who chased the thief is coming back, and he's alone. Perhaps I can find out if he would be willing to give you a description of the man, and what happened when they left me?"

"Yesss, Spider," Simon replied excitedly, "that would be *amazing*. If you get him on the line, I'll be able to record him, do all kinds of analysis on his voice, use it to—"

"I'll do that, then," she said drily, deliberately interrupting him to stop him waffling on about a load of stuff she didn't fully understand. "Please hang on one moment, officer."

She smiled with what she hoped looked like relief as her target reached her. "Wow, hello. I am *so* glad you're all right. I can't believe you did that! Thank you so much, that was so brave." She held out her phone. "I have the police on the telephone right now, and the officer says he would like to speak to you, if possible, to get a description of the man and what happened. It's okay, he speaks *excellent* English." Simon was probably one step ahead of her already and preparing to launch his Dutch accent on their target in order to maintain Mallory's cover.

The man nodded, and held out the bag which contained her sunglasses. "Here you go. Hopefully they're all right. The bastard got fed up of me chasing him and dumped them, so I'm not quite as brave as you think. I didn't have to tackle him or anything. And yes, of course I'll speak to the police." His smile was wide, winning, and Mallory was impressed at how well he was keeping his cool in the face of talking to the authorities. Or so he thought. But then, from what she'd learned about him and his criminal friends so far, they weren't exactly the sort that hid in the shadows. It seemed they were more into hiding in plain sight.

Taking the bag, she then handed him the phone. "Great, thank you."

His brown eyes held hers as he put the handset to his ear. Heat started to rush to her cheeks, so she quickly dropped her gaze, then busied herself with checking to see if the sunglasses had survived their little adventure. They had, fortunately. She usually got to keep anything she purchased on missions like this—taking things back for refunds would attract attention, after all—so it would have been a shame if they'd got broken.

"Yes, hello. I'm the man who gave chase to… actually, I don't know her name… hang on." The man looked at Mallory again, his eyebrows raised in enquiry. "What's your name?"

"Bea Winchester."

A quick nod, and he returned his attention to the phone call. "I'm the man who gave chase to Ms Winchester's thief. My name is Baxter Collinson."

There was a brief pause, whereby Simon was likely "introducing" himself and asking all the right questions.

Baxter Collinson, eh? Now she knew his name, she could apply the information that had been gathered about him to his face, as their hacker had somehow obliterated photo IDs of the whole gang. He was thirty-four years old, Cambridge-educated, born and brought up in a small village outside of Cambridge, and didn't seem to have any kind of employment record. But then, one could hardly put *international jewel thief and forger* on their CV, now, could they? Maybe the gang's computer whizz had tinkered with those records, too.

Baxter wasn't looking at her anymore—he was shifting from foot to foot, taking a pace here and there, glancing at the world passing them by. And they were passing, now. It seemed they were no longer a spectacle, and everything had gone back to normal. She was relieved in a way, but also panicked. How on earth would the team find those people that may have filmed or taken photos of her now? They could be halfway across the city, completely unaware of the sensitive information nestled in their phones' memory.

Shifting her attention back to Baxter, she took the opportunity to examine him close-up. As she'd expected from the upbringing and education, he was every bit as posh as his name implied. His outfit was casual, but still expensive—perhaps he was a fan of the very designer stores she'd been frequenting. His accent was plummy, and he was incredibly attractive, with his short blond hair, brown eyes and trim but strong-looking physique. He was just on the right side of being a pretty boy, in fact.

All of those things, she decided, made him a perfect candidate for his chosen—possibly the wrong choice of word, but it'd do for now—career. He was young, attractive, British upper-class and well-educated. Nobody in their right mind would suspect him of being part of a multi-million-pound international diamond scam. He looked more like he should be working in finance, or modelling. Possibly even just spending the family money and living a life of leisure—which could, actually, be what he'd spent his post-university years doing. That would also explain his spotty employment record.

In his case, though, looks were most definitely deceiving. She knew damn well what he really did for a living, and now was the perfect time to get her claws into him and find out more. The impromptu daylight robbery had thrust them together in a completely unexpected but serendipitous way, saving her the trouble of manufacturing a meeting and hopefully, removing any chance of suspicion on his part. That was, if he was even the suspicious sort. She guessed she'd find out soon enough.

"Yes, I was very close to Ms Winchester when the theft took place," Baxter was saying. "Obviously I wasn't sure what was happening at first. I just saw movement from the corner of my eye, then Ms Winchester began shouting at the man, and for someone to stop him. So I didn't get a good look at his face, as by the time I was paying attention, he already had his back to us, and was running away."

There was a pause.

"Yes, yes, of course. He wore a dark blue hoodie, jeans and black trainers. He had his hood up, so I'm not even sure what colour his hair was. When we were running, he glanced back at me a couple of times, so I got very brief glimpses of his face, though the hood hid much of it. He was white, and given his dark eyebrows, his hair is probably dark. Though for all I know, he could have a shaved head. He's athletic, if his running speed is anything to go by, and is around six feet tall."

Low level sound from the phone's speaker told Mallory that Simon was asking more questions.

"Um, I'm not sure there's much more I can tell you about him physically. I followed him from where he stole Ms Winchester's bag, outside Royal Coster Diamonds. He turned left, towards the canal, then ran parallel with the fencing at the top end of the Vondelpark. When we drew close to the main road, he ditched the shopping bag and dashed in front of a tram. By the time it had gone past, I couldn't see him anywhere. I picked up the bag and looked around for him, but he'd disappeared. I'm sorry I can't be of any more help." Another pause. "Yes, absolutely. No problem. Thank you." He held the phone out to Mallory, who took it back from him with a smile.

"Hello, officer?"

"Hello, Ms Winchester. Is there anything you would like to add to Mr Collinson's statement?"

She subtly shifted a couple of steps away from Baxter to prevent him being able to hear the other end of the conversation. "No, I don't think so. Obviously I could hear what Mr Collinson said, and I don't have any further details on what the thief looked like, unfortunately. But I do have my sunglasses back, so all is not lost! It was very lucky for me that Mr Collinson was nearby."

"Yes." Now it was Simon's turn to adopt a dry tone of voice. "Quite. Can I be frank with you, Ms Winchester?"

She knew what he was really asking. Glancing over at Baxter, she saw he was tapping at his own phone. He was waiting for her, but wasn't trying to overhear what was being said. "Yes, of course."

"Spider, that was excellent. We got a really good sample of his voice, so we'll be able to use it going forward if we're bugging any phone lines he happens to talk on… you get the idea. It was incredibly useful. Now, I'll love you and leave you to do your bit. The team is on standby and can be scrambled within fifteen minutes. Oh, and the footage and photos from the smart phones are already taken care of, so nothing to worry about there. Be careful. Talk to you soon."

"Absolutely. I understand. Thank you so much for your help, officer… yes, I'll be sure to get back in touch if I think of anything else."

"Copy that."

"Goodbye."

Mallory pressed the end call button and put the phone away. Then she looked over at Baxter, trying to figure out the best way to spend some more time with him.

He beat her to it. Grinning, he swiped a hand over his sweaty forehead and said, "All that running's given me quite the appetite. Would you care to go for lunch with me?"

Returning his grin, she nodded. "Yes, that would be lovely. But it's on me. A thank you for being my hero. No arguments."

He rolled his eyes. "Not very gentlemanly, but I can tell you're not a woman to be argued with. Any preference as to where we go?"

She shook her head. "Not really. I eat most foods, so whatever you fancy."

"Sushi?"

"Sushi it is." She allowed him to relieve her of her shopping bags, and took the arm that he offered her. "Thank you. At this rate, I shall be forever in your debt."

Smirking, Baxter replied, "I'm sure we'll think of some way for you to pay me back."

Narrowing her eyes, she shot him a mock-glare. But inside her head, she yelled *Got you.*

Chapter Seven

Less than fifteen minutes later, they were seated at a table by the window in a sushi restaurant. They had an amazing view of the street, and they both glanced out as they sipped at the glasses of cold water that Baxter had just poured for them from the carafe. Their eyes met as they turned their attention back to the table. Mallory smiled and put down her glass. "Like people watching, do you?"

Baxter shrugged. "It's not my main hobby, but it can be kind of interesting at times. Take today—*we* were the ones being watched, causing a spectacle, albeit unintentionally. I suspect people found us *very* interesting."

Nodding, Mallory resisted the temptation to jump in and ask him what his main hobby was. Not like he was going to come right out and say "being a criminal." Instead, she replied, "True. If I'd been a bystander, I'd probably have been gawping at us, too. I have to thank you again for your help, by the way. I know he only got a pair of sunglasses, but still… they're so damn pretty, and a girl's gotta have pretty sunglasses." She grinned, then shot a wry glance at the sky out of the window. "I don't think I'll be needing them today, though."

"No, nor me." He followed her gaze for a moment, where the clouds were darkening once more, and this time Mallory suspected they were well and truly going to burst.

"Ugh!" She lightly slapped the table, drawing Baxter's attention back to her. "Get us, being all British and talking about the weather! Or being on the cusp of it, anyway."

His handsome face lit up with another smile, then he shook his head. "Bloody hell, you're right. We just can't seem to help it, can we?"

"Nope. Terrible habit. It's like it's programmed into our DNA, or something. So I'm going to go out on a limb and completely change the subject, all right?" She pretended to think, her finger coyly pressed to her lips for a moment. Then, "I know. So… aside from people watching, what are your other hobbies? Your main hobby?"

"Oh, you know," he waved a dismissive hand, which, if he hadn't already been a target, would have immediately put her on guard, "the usual. Travelling, reading, films, sports."

"That gives me a lot to go on." She meant it, too. If she'd

been genuinely flirting with the guy, wanting to get to know him, the pastimes he'd listed gave her plenty of scope to go into more detail. The trouble was, it wasn't really his bloody hobbies she wanted to know about. It was how he lined his pockets. But she couldn't jump right in with job questions now—it'd be too suspicious. So she had to continue with her current line of enquiry. She tried not to get disheartened—one never knew what would turn up in conversation when one was least expecting it. Plus, she couldn't complain—she was hardly sitting across the table from a contender for world's ugliest man, was she?

She was prevented from deciding on which topic to pursue by the arrival of a waitress. They placed their orders, then Mallory took another drink before continuing. "All right, since we're both away from home, though admittedly not a million miles away, let's start with travel. What brings you to Amsterdam?"

"On this occasion, it's actually work rather than pleasure. Though admittedly, I do enjoy my job. And getting the opportunity to have lunch with a beautiful woman definitely tilts the scales more towards pleasure. What about you?"

Damn it—he'd answered the question, but fired one right back, meaning she couldn't jump in at the opening about work. *Patience, Mallory. You're going to have to play the slow game here.* She smiled demurely, then dropped firmly into character. Glancing around, she leaned over the table towards him. "Can you keep a secret?"

Baxter's eyes widened momentarily, then he nodded enthusiastically. "Of course."

Lowering her voice, Mallory said, "I'm a luxury lifestyle blogger." Noticing the crease between his eyebrows, she carried on. "I travel to various places all over the world and check out the local businesses—luxury hotels, designer shops, spas, restaurants… you get the idea."

Still frowning, Baxter nodded. "I get what you *do*, but I don't get why it's a secret."

She smiled. "Because I don't want to be treated any differently. How can you really know what a place is like if the staff are pandering to you because they're worried about what you'll write? I want to receive the treatment *every* client receives, meaning I can write honest articles. Yes, it means I probably miss out on lots of perks," she shrugged, "but if it means I can say I had a wonderful experience somewhere and be confident others will too, then it's worth it. Equally, if somewhere is horrible, or the food is bad, or the staff rude, I can warn people off."

Sticking out his bottom lip, Baxter's expression was thoughtful. "Okay, yeah, now I totally get it. You're like a mystery shopper, but not just for shops. I have to say, though, based on what I saw earlier this morning, you do still get *some* perks..." He trailed off and grinned widely, his eyes full of mischief.

Narrowing her eyes, Mallory sat back in her chair and folded her arms. "Can't say it wasn't a perk, but it was nothing to do with my job. Just two consenting adults having a bit of fun together. Why, you jealous?"

He held his hands up. "Hey, don't get all defensive on me. I was just teasing you. And yeah," he ran a hand through his hair and dropped his gaze to the table, "maybe I *am* jealous. What red-blooded male wouldn't be?"

She was saved from having to formulate a response by the arrival of their food. Smiling at the waitress, Mallory said, "This looks great, thank you."

"Yes, thank you," Baxter added.

"You're welcome," the waitress said. "Can I get you anything else to drink?"

"I'm okay with water, thanks. Baxter?"

"No, I'm good too, thank you."

With a nod, the waitress left.

Mallory picked up her chopsticks. "This really *does* look great. I hope it tastes as good as it looks."

"Yeah, me too." Baxter reached for his own chopsticks, and they fell silent for a while as they commenced the tricky task of eating with tiny strips of wood, exchanging the occasional glance and smile over the table.

Mallory used the time wisely, trying to figure out her next move. Fortunately for her—or more accurately, for the mission—it was clear that Baxter was attracted to her. That would certainly make things much easier. She just had to hook him in, then leave him wanting more, try to build on his interest in her so he'd want to see her again, and soon. This part was always a delicate process—go overboard and she could arouse suspicion—but one she'd successfully executed on many occasions, and with much more dangerous criminals than Baxter Collinson.

She shouldn't underestimate him, though. Just because he wasn't a drug or arms dealer, a terrorist or a people trafficker didn't mean he couldn't turn nasty on her if he worked out what was happening. People were often defensive when it came to the things or people they cared about, and he'd already told her how much he enjoyed his job. It was unlikely that anyone that tried to ruin a man's chances of earning ridiculous sums of money was going to be able to walk away completely unscathed.

If she did her job right, though, by the time he realised what was going on, and what her role had been, she'd be long gone, and far out of his reach.

Still, it would never do to be complacent.

They finished up their food at almost the same time, then settled back in their seats, exchanging another grin. "Well," Mallory said, "I'm pleased to say that tasted even better than it looked. Yours?"

Baxter nodded. "Yep. What you said." He rubbed his abdomen. "Dessert?"

He obviously wasn't in any rush to end their lunch date, which she took as a good sign. Seemed her claws were already digging in to him. "Yeah… but not here. I've got a better idea."

"Oh?"

"Do you like chocolate?"

"Is the Pope Catholic? Is the sky blue? Do bears shit in the woods?"

Laughing, it was Mallory's turn to hold up her hands. "All right, all right. You like chocolate. Good—me too. So let me get the bill, and then we'll go find ourselves something sweet to tantalise our taste buds."

Baxter raised his eyebrows, then raked his gaze down her body—or at least the parts of it he could see above the table. "I think I've already found my something sweet," he said lasciviously.

Mallory couldn't help it—she spluttered out a laugh so loud that it drew the momentary attention of a handful of nearby diners. She clapped a hand over her mouth until she could dampen down her mirth. "Sorry… but seriously?" After catching the eye of their waitress, she made the globally understood gesture for the bill. The waitress nodded, and Mallory turned back to Baxter with a wry grin. "Do those kinds of lines usually work for you? Because it was *terrible!*"

Abashed, Baxter peered at his empty plate for a moment, before making what looked like a gargantuan effort to meet her eyes. "Sorry. It just kind of slipped out. Probably one of those thoughts I should have kept inside my head, eh?" He mock-pouted and gave her puppy-dog eyes. "Do I still get chocolate?"

"Only if you promise you won't spin me any more of those horrendous lines. You might have been my hero today, but that doesn't mean you get to take liberties with the English language, all right?"

"No, ma'am," he said, rearranging his features into a sensible, well-behaved expression. "No more liberties with the English language, no more horrendous lines. No more lines, full stop. You have my word."

"All right. Very good."

The waitress slipped a leather-bound wallet onto their table. Without even looking at the bill, Mallory got her purse out and handed the waitress her—well, Bea Winchester's—credit card with a murmur of thanks. The waitress popped it into the wireless card machine she already held, pressed a few buttons, then handed it back to Mallory, who entered her pin and pushed the OK button. "There you go, thank you."

A few seconds later, the machine spat out a receipt, which the woman tore off and handed to Mallory, along with her credit card. "Thank you very much for your custom, I hope you enjoyed your meals. Please come again."

"We did, thank you. And we will."

With that, the waitress left again, and Mallory and Baxter stood, grabbed their things—Baxter sweeping up most of her shopping bags before she got chance—and headed for the door.

"Thank you for that, Bea, it was delicious."

"You're very welcome. It was the least I could do."

He grinned and strode in front of her to open the door. Just as he gripped the handle, though, it was like a switch had been flipped. The clouds decided now was the perfect time to let rip. For a couple of seconds, it seemed like regular rain, but then it increased in intensity, bucketing down with a ferocity which left Mallory and Baxter staring out at the street, speechless.

Releasing the door handle, Baxter turned around to face Mallory, his eyes wide. "Holy shit! I really want some chocolate!"

Mallory giggled. "Crap. Yeah, I do too." By now, there were

some other people behind them, waiting to leave the restaurant, but because of the cloudburst, no one was in a particular rush to head outside. She smiled politely at them, then looked at Baxter. "Shall we give it a couple of minutes, see if it calms down a bit? The shop I'm thinking of isn't far away, it's just," she glanced down at her feet, "I'm not really wearing the right footwear for running, never mind in the rain."

"No…" Baxter peered thoughtfully at her footwear. "They're not really designed for running, are they? Though, and this isn't a line, merely an observation, they are great shoes."

"Thank you. So, are we waiting?"

"Naturally. Though I've got to say, teasing me with luxury chocolate, then making me wait for it is a risky move. I'm starting to get the shakes."

"There, there." She patted him playfully on the head. "Be patient. It'll be worth the wait, I promise."

"Well, when you put it like that…"

Chapter Eight

Mallory and Baxter got some strange looks as they hurried through the hotel foyer towards the lifts, shivering and dripping water on the marble floors as they went.

Baxter stabbed at the button to call the elevator, and turned to Mallory, forcing a smile past his chattering teeth. "Bloody hell, talk about biblical rain. Don't get me wrong, I love this city, but back in London, at least we'd have been able to hail a cab. They're hard to find here—easier to hail a bike!"

"Wouldn't have made a difference. We were on a pedestrianised street."

"Oh yeah. Duh. Damn it! Where's the lift, I'm freezing!"

He looked it, too. Despite his cheesy chat up lines, he was a gentleman and had given her his sweater. Naturally, it wasn't waterproof, so didn't help her that much, but it was the thought that counted. They'd grown bored of waiting for the rain to lessen, so Mallory had retrieved her umbrella, reluctantly accepted his sweater, and they'd hurried as fast as her heels would allow out of the sushi restaurant and down the road to the chocolate shop, cursing and giggling all the way. The rain was practically horizontal, and so fierce that it bounced from the pavements, so the umbrella was pointless. A boat would have been more useful.

Already soaked, they grew cold and so didn't linger in the shop, allowing the assistant to pack them up a selection of their most popular confections, before paying and heading back to the hotel.

After what felt like an age, the lift arrived and they stepped in. Baxter selected the button for their floor and they waited in silence as they were transported. Mallory figured that if she wasn't so damn cold and uncomfortable, she'd actually have appreciated the wet T-shirt look on Baxter. The material had gone almost see-through and clung to his athletic body like a second skin. She stored away the mental image for a later date, when she wasn't a shivering, drowned rat.

When the doors slid open with a mechanical hiss, they hurried out and in the direction of their rooms, Mallory already rooting in her bag for her key card. Locating it, she clutched it in her icy cold fist, ready to open her room door, dump her stuff and jump in the shower as quickly as possible.

They stopped at her door. With her fingers shaking as they

were, it took a couple of attempts to unlock it, but she got there eventually. Pushing open the door, she turned to Baxter, taking the shopping bags he proffered. "Thank you so much for lending me your sweater. I'll bring it back to you as soon as I've showered and changed."

"No need. I'll come and collect it when *I've* showered and changed."

"You will, will you?" She raised her eyebrows at his presumptuousness.

He grinned. "Come on… have some pity on a bloke. I was your hero, then I lent you my sweater and got soaked to the skin for the sake of some luxury chocolates. I've had a traumatic day. Surely you won't deprive me of the chocolate I walked in a deluge to get? You talked it up so much!"

Mallory shook her head, smirking at his little-boy-lost tone. "You're right. I apologise. Of *course* I won't deprive you. I'm not that cruel. Though I was right there with you in the deluge, I hasten to point out, sweater or no sweater. Go get yourself sorted out, then come back and we'll dig into the chocolates."

Baxter's smile widened. "Excellent. I'll bring something complementary." He winked.

"I look forward to it. Now *go.*"

"Yes, ma'am." Still smiling, he turned and headed for his own room. She still wasn't sure exactly which one it was, but figured at this point, it didn't really matter.

Cold as she was, Mallory didn't stop to enjoy the view. She dashed through the door, slammed it, and headed for the bedroom. Once there, she dropped everything in her hands onto the bed. Kicking off her shoes, she then jogged to the bathroom, stripping as she went.

Soon, she was standing under the blissfully hot spray, still shivering slightly as the chill seeped out of her. She remained standing there for a while, not even attempting to clean up until her skin felt warm again. When it finally did, she heaved a sigh of relief. She hated being cold. She made quick work of washing and rinsing her hair and body, then switched off the shower and got out.

Having wrapped her hair up into a towel, she shrugged into the luscious fluffy hotel bathrobe and headed back to the bedroom to get dressed.

She'd just laid her chosen outfit out on her bed, then towel dried and brushed her hair, when a knock came at the main door. *Shit!* That couldn't be Baxter already? Looking around at the mess that was her bedroom—not to mention the devastation she'd left behind on her way to the shower—and taking in to consideration the fact she wasn't even dressed, she walked towards the door and called out, "Who is it?"

There was a pause. Mallory could just picture Baxter's handsome face scrunching up into a frown as he wondered who the hell else she could be expecting. "It's me… Baxter."

"Just a minute! I'm only just out of the shower."

"That's okay. I don't mind."

Smiling, she shook her head, wondering why she was even bothered about the mess and her state of undress. She was looking to intrigue the guy, sink her claws into him and pump him for information, not marry him. And given what had happened that morning, which already felt like a lifetime ago, he knew she was no angel. Acting coy now just seemed pointless. "Just give me one minute, okay?"

She didn't wait for a reply. Instead, she rushed around and tried to make the place at least half presentable—snatching up all the sodden clothes she'd abandoned and dumping them in the shower tray. She'd call down to Reception later and arrange to have them laundered.

She walked back over to the door and peered through the peephole on instinct. As she'd expected, he was alone. If, by some miracle, he'd sussed out who she was and what she was up to, he was hardly going to turn up at her door in the middle of the day and kill her, was he?

Rolling her eyes at her own stupidity, she opened the door. "Hey. Sorry to keep you waiting, I just had to have a bit of a tidy up. It took longer than I expected to thaw out in the shower. Come in." She stepped back and allowed him access, taking in his attire—another pair of well-fitting jeans, smart shoes and a navy blue T-shirt. Since they were indoors, he clearly didn't feel the need for a sweater. Or perhaps his only one was currently sitting in a state of sodden-ness in her shower. His blond hair was still damp, and she ignored the tug low in her belly that signalled her attraction to him.

"No worries. I probably should have waited a bit longer before coming over. What can I say, I couldn't resist the siren call of luxury chocolate. And, as promised, I brought a little something to go with it." He brandished a bottle of champagne and two glasses. "Shall I pour while you get dressed? Or, you know, you could stay like that…"

She shot him a dirty look. "Go ahead and pour. I'll only be a couple of minutes." She retrieved the clean clothes she'd left in the bedroom and went into the bathroom to get ready.

Once the door was securely closed behind her, she scrambled to make herself presentable. Within her allotted two minutes she'd pulled on underwear, jeans and a pretty blouse—all designer, of course—and had put some product into her hair so that she could allow it to dry naturally without ending up looking like a scarecrow. She could cope with Baxter seeing her *au naturel,* but she didn't want to scare him away by being too careless with her looks.

When she walked back out into the lounge area, Baxter was sitting on one of the sofas, just topping off the champagne glasses. She'd heard the pop of the cork as she'd been getting ready. She flashed him a smile. "Mmm, yummy. Let me just find the chocolates."

"I thought about looking for them, but I didn't want to go into your bedroom and dig around in your shopping."

She wasn't sure how to respond to that, so she didn't bother, silently thankful that he hadn't rooted around. Knowing her luck, he'd have found the sexy lingerie before he found the chocolates, and judging by the way he flirted with her and made his occasional saucy comments, he wouldn't be able to keep quiet about his discovery. He'd probably try and persuade her to model them for him.

That wasn't necessarily a bad thing, but she had to maintain a careful balance. It was okay to let Baxter think she was attracted to him, and that she'd like something to happen between them—not that either of those points were a *complete* fabrication—but at the same time, he couldn't be allowed to come to the conclusion that she was a pushover. That might turn him off, or bore him, and if he lost interest in her, her mission was in trouble. She couldn't exactly just latch on to one of the other men in the gang—that would definitely set alarm bells ringing.

She went to the bedroom and located the confectionary. As she re-entered the sitting room, she waved the bag triumphantly and headed over to where he sat, taking the seat opposite. Putting the goodies on the table between them, she then picked up her glass.

"Thank you so much for bringing champagne, Baxter. What a great idea."

Snagging his own glass, he smiled and shrugged. "You paid for lunch and bought the chocolates. I was feeling a bit emasculated."

Rolling her eyes, Mallory leaned forward and held out her champagne flute. "To retrieving stolen designer sunglasses, and eating posh chocolates and drinking bubbly in the middle of the day."

With a nod, Baxter touched the rim of his glass to hers. "Cheers, Bea."

"Cheers." She took a tiny, slow sip. In a display of freakish déjà-vu from the previous evening with Erasmus, her subconscious was working overtime—making her wonder if he could have poisoned it, or drugged it. Baxter Collinson, after all, was *not* just a waiter and barman. He was a criminal, so would poisoning or drugging someone be so far out of his wheelhouse? Trying hard to shove her concerns aside—she'd heard the cork pop, after all—she put down the glass and set about removing the confectionary from the bag. She'd bought a large box which the member of staff in the shop said contained truffles, bon bons, pralines and similar titbits of varying flavours. Basically, as long as you weren't allergic to nuts, gluten or dairy, which she and Baxter had both confirmed they weren't, there was something nestled in the box for every taste.

She untied the silky red ribbon, lifted the lid, removed the layer of paper and gasped as the contents were revealed.

"Bloody hell," Baxter quipped, a smirk taking over his lips, "the last time I heard a woman make a noise like that, I'd just found her G-spot."

She raised her eyebrows and gave him a pointed look, while inside she couldn't help but be amused by his incessant cheekiness. "Aren't you supposed to be behaving yourself? Any more of that and I'll rescind my offer to share my chocolates with you."

Clutching his heart theatrically, he replied, "You wound me! You wouldn't do such a thing, surely? And who said anything about behaving myself? I promised not to keep spinning you cheesy lines, and I've kept that promise. That wasn't a line, merely stating a fact. Maybe you just don't want me to talk at all. Maybe you just want some eye candy in your hotel room to look at while you drink champagne and eat truffles in the middle of the day. Speaking of which… why *are* we doing this in the middle of the day? Don't you have work to do?"

"Don't *you* have work to do?" she shot back. "Who are you, my boss?"

"Touché." He took a sip of champagne. "I don't have what you'd call a nine-to-five job. I'm not working until tonight. What's your excuse?"

"Well, my job isn't nine-to-five, either. And technically, I *have* been working since I left the hotel this morning. I've visited lots of designer shops, a diamond shop, a sushi restaurant and a chocolatier. All of that is very valuable research."

"And will you be mentioning the man who rescued your designer sunglasses from an opportunistic thief in your article?"

"It's a fascinating story, but I don't think it really fits in with what I'm trying to do with the piece." Seeing his disappointed expression, she decided to throw him a bone. "Besides, maybe I want to keep my brave, sunglasses-saving hero as my sexy little secret? Maybe I don't want to share him?"

Chapter Nine

Baxter's grin turned wicked. "Now you're just trying to flatter me."

"And? Is it working?"

He languidly shrugged one shoulder. "Dunno. Depends what you're after, I suppose…"

Shit. She was trying not to allow things to move too quickly between them, but it didn't seem to be working. The flirtation kept winning out, their apparent chemistry doing battle with her sensible side—and winning.

"Chocolate?" she said brightly, snatching up the box and thrusting it in his direction.

He narrowed his eyes at her for a fraction of a second, probably fully aware that she was changing the subject. Then he smiled and reached towards the box. "I thought you'd never ask. Hmm… what have we got here then?" He snagged a miniature stick of dark chocolate and slipped it between his lips, then bit it in half.

Mallory watched, transfixed, as Baxter let the chocolate melt in his mouth for a few moments, before beginning to chew. An expression of bliss had taken over his face, and a rumble of pleasure came from deep within his chest. Moisture gathered in her mouth and between her legs as she simultaneously anticipated chocolate in the former, and Baxter—tongue, fingers or cock—in the latter.

Bloody hell. The chocolate wasn't the only thing in the vicinity that was melting.

In a desperate attempt to distract herself, she nabbed a chocolate before returning the box to the table. Popping the tiny round confection into her mouth, she instinctively closed her eyes as her taste buds were blissfully assaulted. She hadn't even looked to see what she'd picked up, but she now knew it was a salted caramel, and *holy shit* it was good! The mixture of sweetness and saltiness, the delicious, high-quality chocolate, was sublime, and it had well and truly done its job of distracting her from dirty thoughts of Baxter and his sinful lips.

In spite of her taking her time, letting the caramel melt in her mouth, bathing her tongue with flavour, it was over all too soon. Pouting, she opened her eyes, wanting a sip of champagne to wash it down with before sampling something else. But as soon as she lifted her lids, her gaze collided with Baxter's. He wore an expression that she suspected mirrored the one she'd worn when she'd watched him eat his first chocolate. His eyelids were heavy with lust, his pupils wide, his lips slightly parted. He stared at her a moment longer, the tiny frown line that appeared between his eyebrows indicating he was fighting some indecision at what to do or say next.

"Good, huh?" he finally managed, before licking his lips. A slight flush dotted his cheeks.

Unconsciously, she copied him, then mentally kicked herself. *So much for not flirting!* She forced a smile. "Yes. Totally delicious. Yours?"

"Likewise. Though the word delicious doesn't seem to do it justice."

"I couldn't agree more. Another?" Without waiting for a response, she slid the box towards him, then picked up her glass for another drink. God, if only she wasn't on the job. She'd love to be able to get drunk, or even tipsy—just enough to dull her senses, to stop her being so damn aware of him, of what he was doing to her, whether he was doing it intentionally or not.

She took a mouthful of champagne, enjoying the fizzing sensation as the bubbles popped on her tongue.

Baxter was peering into the box, apparently unable to decide which treat he wanted to sample next. She put down her glass and leaned forward with a smile. "Can't make up your mind?"

"Nope. I'm literally spoilt for choice here."

Seeing an opportunity to lighten the mood, and dispel some of the atmosphere between them, she replied, "Why don't I help you?"

His response was a quirked eyebrow.

"Close your eyes."

He did.

Reaching over, she took hold of his wrist and guided his hand towards the box, then began making random patterns over the top of it—round and round, up and down, left and right, figures of eight. Then, realising the sensation of his warm skin beneath hers was doing little to dull the increasing ache between her legs, she positioned his hand over a truffle and gently pushed down before releasing him. "There you go."

Fumbling only slightly, he closed his fingers around the truffle and pulled it from the box. Opening his eyes, he smiled at her. "Thank you. Mmm… good choice. I love truffles. But then, you've probably worked out by now that I love anything sweet."

"I think I'll have one, too." She spotted an identical truffle and picked it up. "Try them together?"

He nodded and held it in front of his mouth.

Mallory did the same. "In three?"

Baxter nodded again.

Together, they counted down. "Three… two… *one*."

Simultaneously popping the confections between their lips, they maintained eye contact as they ate. That turned out to be the biggest mistake of all. As they savoured their respective truffles, they were each watching the other enjoy *theirs,* too. It was a continuous cycle of pleasure, one that seemed to fill the room with an indescribable yet palpable force, one that stretched and expanded until it threatened to burst out of the windows in a hail of shattered glass.

Mallory's heart pounded. In her panic, she struggled to swallow the last of the morsel. Aided by some more of the bubbly, she finally managed it, and peered sheepishly over at Baxter. He now looked serious, *too* serious, and her heart rate kicked up another notch. She looked away. This *thing*—whatever it was—between them was clearly affecting him, too. But what was he going to do about it? He had no reason to hold back. God, if an international diamond thief and smuggler couldn't take what he wanted, when he wanted it, then who the hell could?

She was frozen with indecision, an impotent state that happened to her rarely and frustrated her immensely. Part of her skill set was the ability to make decisions, even tough ones, at the drop of a hat, as often she simply didn't have the luxury of time to think about it. Granted, she had a little bit of time now—no one was holding a gun to her head, after all. But the trouble was, on this occasion, she didn't have enough information to make an informed decision. If she had sex with Baxter Collinson now, how would it affect the situation? Would it leave him wanting more, or, because he'd gotten what he wanted, would he disappear? Equally, if she didn't sleep with him, would he think she was just a flirt, a cocktease, and walk away?

She'd never deliberated so hard about fucking someone in her entire life. It was bizarre—especially since she, Mallory Scott, very much *wanted* to fuck him. But it wasn't about Mallory Scott and her wants. It was about Bea Winchester, luxury lifestyle blogger, and getting enough information about the illicit diamond dealing gang to take down the operation and put the perpetrators away for a very long time.

Mallory bit her lip. Damn, she almost felt sorry for him. He was way too pretty to go to prison. Unless he played his cards right, or had the right kind of contacts on the inside, he'd be someone's bitch within a week.

Baxter cleared his throat, snapping her out of her troubled thoughts and focusing her attention firmly back onto him. Shifting forwards on the sofa, he said, "Uh… I think I should probably go."

"What?" she squeaked. "I mean, er, oh! Sorry, I didn't realise I was keeping you… I thought you didn't have to work until tonight."

"I don't," he replied with a frown. "But… I dunno… things got weird and I thought perhaps you wanted me to leave."

"No, not at all." She shook her head.

"Oh." His frown deepened. "I must have gotten the wrong idea, then. I thought there was something between us, to be honest. I thought you were flirting with me. Then you kept changing the subject, then you went all quiet… I thought you were blowing me off. If you'll pardon the pun."

The laugh bubbled out before she could stop it. "Pun pardoned. No, I wasn't *blowing you off.* Not really. I was just… well…" *Ah, fuck it. In for a penny, in for a pound.* "I don't want you to think I'm some kind of slut."

Baxter's eyebrows shot up. "And why would I think that?"

"Well, after this morning…" She fidgeted in her seat and twisted her hands together, only half-acting her discomfort. "What you saw. The barman—waiter, whatever. And then if I… with you…" She forced herself to meet his gaze, then shrugged.

He shrugged right back. "You're a free agent, aren't you?"

Mallory's stomach lurched uncomfortably at his far-too-close-to-the-bone choice of words, but she didn't react outwardly. "Yes. The barman—Erasmus—was just a bit of fun. I don't make a habit of it, though. You won't tell anyone, will you?" She threw in the plan she'd formulated earlier, hoping it would make her seem more genuine.

"Tell anyone? Like who?"

"Like someone at the hotel. I don't want to get Erasmus into trouble. He's a nice guy."

"Of course I'm not going to tell anyone, Bea! What happened is none of my business. And when it comes to us, well, I'm an adult, you're an adult, we're both unattached, and now we're having an incredibly awkward, somewhat embarrassing conversation. What could possibly be more erotic?"

She smiled. "A sense of humour in a guy is pretty damn erotic."

"Glad I've got something going for me."

"Yeah. It's about the only thing." She bit back a smirk.

"That so? That's a very hurtful thing to say. You know…" He slid his gaze to the box on the table. "I think I might just have to go and cry in the corner and eat that entire box of chocolates to make myself feel better."

Quickly figuring out his next move, Mallory made a grab for the box, but she was a millisecond too slow. Baxter had snagged it, and now he jumped up from the sofa and moved a few paces away, holding it aloft, his height and long arms meaning it was well out of her reach. She tried nonetheless, getting up and running over to him, then stretching up to try and retrieve the chocolates.

Laughing, he danced away from her. "Serves you right for hurting my feelings. If you want them back, you have to make me feel better."

"Oh yeah?" She stopped and jammed her hands on her hips, fixing him with a narrow-eyed stare. "And how do you propose I do that? As if I couldn't guess…" She rolled her eyes good-naturedly.

"How about a kiss?" He lowered the box, tucked it behind his back and puckered his lips. After giving her a pointed glance, he closed his eyes.

Mallory couldn't help but smile. The man was completely incorrigible. His silliness was infectious, and she ached to throw caution to the wind and have a bit of stupid fun with him. Fool around. Laugh until her stomach hurt and tears ran down her face. It'd be so easy to do that with him, and no doubt would be the quickest way to gain his confidence.

With that thought, her decision was made. She wouldn't lower her guard entirely—that was suicide, either literally or of the career kind at the very least—but she'd allow herself to have some genuine fun. With the ultimate goal of intelligence gathering, of course. If she happened to have some great sex along the way, then so much the better.

Closing the space between them, Mallory slipped her hand behind Baxter's neck and drew him down to her level. Then she planted one on him. It was chaste to begin with—the sort of gesture reserved for a friend or family member—but she quickly found she couldn't pull away. Or didn't want to.

As the seconds ticked on and neither of them moved, Mallory knew what she had to do next. Baxter hadn't the slightest idea of the deliberation and angsting that had been going on in her head, much less of the decision she'd eventually come to. For all he knew, she was simply playing along with his game, planning to give him the kiss he'd requested and be done with it.

Knowing that actions speak much louder than words, Mallory looped her arms around his neck and deepened the kiss, pressing her lips harder to his. When he didn't balk, she tilted her head, opened her mouth and poked out her tongue. Baxter allowed her access willingly, enthusiastically, even.

And when he started to respond, Mallory melted all over again, the chocolate entirely forgotten.

Chapter Ten

It was probably just as well she wasn't really a luxury lifestyle blogger, because Baxter's kissing technique was definitely worth writing about. He'd go viral if he was put online. Settling his free hand into the small of her back, he hauled her up against him, firmly but not forcefully. The lips she'd so admired were warm and soft, and Mallory hummed happily as his tongue slipped against hers. He explored her mouth confidently, without being over the top, ramping up her arousal with every movement.

It wasn't long before she became aware of a hard bulge pressing against her lower stomach. An involuntary growl of need escaped her throat and was swallowed into his mouth.

Almost immediately, Baxter released her and stepped back, looking shell-shocked. He stared at her, wide-eyed, and seemingly lost for words. After a beat, he ran a hand through his hair, then spoke. "Bloody hell. Do you, er… because I, er..." He huffed out a breath and glanced down at his crotch, where his cock made apparent the meaning of the words he hadn't managed to formulate.

Biting her bottom lip, Mallory nodded emphatically. "Put those bloody chocolates down, would you?" She turned and walked into the bedroom without waiting for his response, and hurriedly cleared all her shopping bags off the bed, dumping them on a chair in the corner.

Baxter appeared soon after, empty-handed.

Their gazes met, heat sparking between them, but silence reigned for several long moments. Then the spell broke, and they both began undressing like it was a race.

Mallory was so eager to get her clothes off and feel Baxter's naked skin against hers that she focused only on herself and what she was doing, trying to do it as quickly as possible. Therefore, she didn't get any kind of a tease—no peeking at slices of skin as they were revealed, no imagining what certain body parts would look like before she set her eyes on them.

Instead, once she'd rendered herself bare, she shot a glance across to where Baxter stood on the other side of the bed, and took him all in at once. He did exactly the same to her. And apparently, she wasn't the only one who really liked what she saw. A heartbeat passed; then another.

On the third, they all but pounced onto the bed, meeting in

the middle, and reached for each other. Arousal had taken over, short-circuiting their brains and leaving their bodies and sexual cravings in complete control.

As their lips met, Baxter immediately took the dominant position, rolling on top of Mallory and possessing her mouth. She melted into the embrace, taking advantage of the opportunity to let her hands wander over his heated skin, tracing the fine muscles of his back, dipping into the curve of his spine, then sweeping down to the mounds of his buttocks. Squeezing them hard, she smiled internally as he jerked and let out a yelp, then kissed her more roughly, whipping them both up into a frenzy.

Her actions had also brought his cock within a hair's breadth of her pussy. It was dangerously close, and her need to have him inside her was strong, almost overwhelming. Retaining just enough presence of mind to avoid a stupid mistake, she forced her hand between their bodies and gripped his shaft. Stroking it slowly, she revelled in how it felt in her hand—hard, hot, eager. There wouldn't be much foreplay here, she was sure of it. Or maybe their flirtation over sushi, champagne and chocolate *had* been their foreplay—drawn out over a few hours, keeping them on the edge of need for so long that their final approach towards consummating their mutual attraction was, by necessity, compressed. But not rushed. Rushed implied carelessness, and there was nothing careless about the way he was touching her, and she him.

Baxter had propped his weight on his forearms, which were positioned on either side of her shoulders. His hands cupped her jaw, his thumbs and fingers stroking her face and neck, titillating the sensitive areas even as his lips and tongue continued to plunder her mouth. He was doing a pretty good job of staying focused, despite her increased grip on his cock, though she could tell she was getting to him, as he grew ever harder and thicker in her hand.

Not that he knew it, but her pussy was reacting in kind, getting slicker by the second, her clit swelling almost painfully. She wasn't sure how much longer she could wait. She ached for him in a way that, deep down, she knew she shouldn't, but since when could humans control their sexual urges? They could ignore them, sure, but not make them go away.

After several more glorious minutes of kissing and caressing, Mallory cracked. Twisting her head to one side and breaking their kiss, she gasped for much-needed air, then said, "Please. I need…"

Seemingly afflicted with the lack of words Baxter had experienced not so long ago, she blinked stupidly, then gestured towards the bedside table. "Condom."

Dropping a quick kiss onto her forehead, he then complied. He scrambled over to the edge of the mattress and sat, then opened the drawer of the bedside table and retrieved a foil square. The angle he was sitting at meant she couldn't see what he was doing, but she recognised the sounds of him opening the wrapper and sheathing himself. It took a fair amount of willpower for her not to beg him to hurry. She clenched her fists to try to alleviate some of the frustration, but it made little difference.

Within a minute, though, Baxter was back. His warm, luscious body covered hers as he settled between her spread legs once more. His grin was wide, the look in his eyes wicked. Returning the grin, Mallory reached for him with her arms and legs, pulling him onto her and locking her hands behind his neck and her ankles behind his back.

"Whoa, there," Baxter said, raising his eyebrows. "Nice as it is to be crushed up against your delectable body, it doesn't exactly allow for much finesse, does it?"

Mallory shrugged. "I'm not looking for finesse. I just want to fuck."

"Bloody hell, Bea. Do you have any idea how much most men would love to hear a woman say something like that?"

"I don't care about most men. I'm not naked in bed with most men. I'm naked in bed with *you*. Can we stop talking now, please?"

"Certainly. But, just so you know, I'm not a selfish lover. So even 'just fucking' in my book involves ensuring the lady's pleasure."

Now it was Mallory's turn to raise her eyebrows. "Er, what happened to the not talking?"

Baxter opened his mouth to respond, then seemingly thought better of it and snapped it closed again. Mallory felt a little bad for telling him off, particularly given their intimate predicament, but when he leaned down and captured her mouth in a smouldering kiss, she stopped feeling anything except pleasure. His tongue immediately slipped past her lips and began exploring. At the same time, despite his bemoaning the lack of finesse, he managed, with a bit of hip-wriggling, to position the head of his cock against her entrance. Then, with one long, smooth stroke, he pushed inside.

They both groaned at the sensation, and Mallory gripped him tighter, unwilling to have even a sliver of space between their bodies. He just felt so damn good—on top of her, against her, inside her… everything. She was being driven entirely by lust, and once she'd had a moment to savour his cock filling her, she bucked her hips. Her movement was limited by his weight on top of her, but all she was trying to do was convey her needs without words. She didn't even want to break their kiss, which grew rougher and more frenzied by the second, to tell him what she wanted. She just had to hope he got the hint.

He did. And it quickly became apparent that she wasn't the only one being driven entirely by lust. After a couple of tentative thrusts, presumably to make sure he wasn't hurting her, Baxter immediately launched into a frantic pace, his hips slamming so hard against hers that she just knew she'd ache tomorrow. *Ache so good.* The heat between them quickly turned molten, and the rude sounds of Baxter's cock pounding her soaked pussy filled the room.

He'd managed to angle himself so that with each jerk of his hips, his pubic bone gave her clit a hearty stroke. She canted her own hips, meeting him thrust for thrust. Sparks ignited between her legs, the flames licking out to her abdomen, and gradually taking over her entire body. She felt like one big nerve ending, being stimulated to the extreme, and she knew it wouldn't be long before Baxter's frantic, yet talented, technique tipped her over the edge.

She reluctantly broke their kiss as their passion increased. Her lips felt bruised, swollen, and they tingled as she parted them. She breathed heavily, still hanging on tightly to Baxter, still bucking as he thrust them closer and closer to their respective peaks.

Soon, a tightening in her abdomen warned of her impending climax. "Oh God, I'm getting close…"

"Good, good. Come for me, sweet Bea. I want to feel you come around my cock, feel you squeeze me, feel your juices coat my dick."

His dirty words added further fuel to her erotic fire, setting her off with a yell, followed by a string of expletives. Pleasure slammed into her like a tsunami, lifting her high, carrying her along on tumultuous waves of bliss, before dumping her down, wrung out and trembling.

She was vaguely aware of Baxter's exclamation. "Oh, wow.

That's so… uhh… tight. So good… oh God!"

Apparently her orgasm had drawn out Baxter's own, and he gave a few more deep, fierce thrusts, followed by a bunch of short, sharp ones, before freezing, his cock buried inside her. His shaft twitched repeatedly against her sensitive inner walls, then he dropped his face into the pillow beside her head, moaning and swearing as his climax overwhelmed him.

Eventually he rolled off her, and gazed at her with a cheesy grin on his face. "Well, that was…"

"Yeah," she replied, "it was. Now come here."

"One minute." He got off the bed and walked—a little unsteadily, she thought—out of the room. He returned less than a minute later, minus the condom, and settled down beside her, laying his head on her chest. She basked quietly in her afterglow, waiting to see what happened next. Maybe some post-coital pillow talk would give her the opportunity to tease some information out of him.

Chapter Eleven

The sound of a voice woke Mallory up. She panicked for a second, wondering who the hell was in her room, but then she remembered. Baxter. She hadn't intended to fall asleep, especially not with him still in bed with her, but as her brain slowly started to kick into gear, she realised it could be exactly the break she'd been waiting for.

Carefully cracking one eyelid open, she looked in the direction Baxter's voice was coming from. He'd pulled on his boxer shorts—more was the pity—and was over by the window, his back to her. That, at least, was a good thing. For the moment, he had no idea she was awake and listening to his end of the conversation.

Closing her eye again, she feigned sleep even as her ears pricked, straining to hear his murmured words.

He paused for a moment—maybe turning around to check on her—then carried on talking. "No, I think we should stick with the original plan. Like the boss keeps telling us, the more last minute the final arrangements are, the better. There's less time for any information to leak out. If someone has got loose lips, by the time the authorities find out what we're up to, we'll be halfway to Madagascar. Not that I think anyone would talk, but one can't be too careful."

Silence, presumably as the person at the other end of the phone replied. Baxter listened, then spoke again. "Okay, yeah. If you could let the others know we're a go for tonight. I will go and do some final recon, just to double check everything and make sure we don't get any surprises." A pause. "Yeah, I know that's what I said, but just after we spoke, something came up and I couldn't do it. It's fine. I can be there in twenty minutes. I'll meet you at the RV at eleven. Okay, see you then."

He fell quiet again then, so she assumed he'd ended the call.

She concentrated on keeping her breathing slow and steady, so if he came close enough, he'd think she was still fast asleep. She'd just got her hands on the last piece of the puzzle. The when. She hadn't expected it to be quite so soon. The gang had only arrived in the city a couple of days ago, prompting her to follow them. But from what she'd just overheard, last minute plans were a big part of what kept them safe. Like her, they could research their targets, find out everything they possibly could, their strengths, their weaknesses, all from a distance. So actually, it made perfect sense to steer well clear of the hotspot until it was absolutely necessary to be there—in other words, when the job was imminent.

It also explained why they'd been so elusive up until now. The reason she and her employers hadn't been able to get one step ahead of them was because they didn't give them *time*. How could information be gleaned and leaks exploited if nobody actually knew the pertinent details until the very last minute?

No matter. She had them now. All she had to do was mobilise the team, get them in place, and as soon as Baxter and his buddies were in the thick of their criminal act, they'd swoop in and take them down. Once they were in custody, they'd be questioned, and at least one member of the group was bound to crack. In exchange for a reduced sentence, or some other kind of deal, they'd dish the dirt on their partners in crime. That, coupled with legislation allowing her organisation to search properties, and access phone and online records, meant that they'd soon have more than enough evidence, not only to put them away for the crime they'd been caught committing, but to charge them with earlier ones, too. By the time she and the team were done, they'd all be going away for a very long time.

As the mattress dipped beside her, she felt a pang of regret. She knew how ridiculous it was—he might be cute, and a great lay, but no one was holding a gun to his head and making him take part in an international diamond scam. He'd told her himself that he enjoyed his job. Just because he wasn't physically hurting people, or selling products that hurt people, didn't mean he wasn't a bad guy. He was smart—smart enough to know how his actions would affect the businesses and industry he and his buddies targeted. There was no such thing as a victimless crime, not really.

All of that was irrelevant, anyway. It didn't matter how she felt about Baxter, about his crimes, and how he'd ended up doing what he did. What mattered was that he was on the verge of being put away, and being punished for what he'd done. It was a big win for the team, especially since she'd been put into play expecting the operation to take quite a while. Instead, a series of unexpected events meant she'd got the required information in little over twenty-four hours.

But, she reminded herself, she shouldn't count her chickens until they'd hatched. Right now, Baxter wasn't behind bars. He was on the bed next to her, stroking her hair and murmuring at her to wake up. There was still a ways to go before she could say this mission had been a success.

"Hmm?" she said lazily, keeping her eyes closed. She stretched her limbs, turning her head away from Baxter, opening her eyes and giving them a moment to focus, then shifting to face him. "Oh, hello," she murmured with a grin. "Sorry, I didn't mean to fall asleep. You must have worn me out."

He returned her grin. "I'll take that as a compliment. Don't worry, though. I wore myself out, too. We've both been asleep for a while. Which means I've got to rush off. Remember I said I have to work tonight?"

"Aww..." Mallory pouted. "Just think of the fun we could have been having instead of sleeping." The last part, at least, was true. The first part was bullshit—far from being disappointed he was leaving, she could hardly wait to be rid of him. As soon as he was gone, she had to hurry up and orchestrate the strategy that would result in his arrest.

Baxter ruffled her hair affectionately. "Yeah, tell me about it. And unfortunately I'm leaving town as soon as I'm done working, too. But if our schedules match up, maybe we can hook up in London sometime? You know, if you want to." He sounded hopeful, yet unsure, and another pang hit her.

Good God, she needed to get a grip. Was she losing her fucking touch, or what? She'd never had any problems divorcing sex and emotion before. Why was this guy any different? Fucking him had been the means to an end—nothing more.

With that in mind, she lied through her teeth. "Yeah, that would be great." She leaned over and kissed him. "I'll grab my phone before I see you out, and we can exchange numbers. Seems we're both pretty busy, but hopefully we'll be able to figure something out."

"All right. Sounds good."

They dressed in silence, and Baxter waited by the door as she dug around in her bag to retrieve her phone. Once she found it, she quickly unlocked it and pulled up the screen to enter a new contact. She typed in his name and showed him. "Did I spell your surname right?"

She knew damn well she had, but figured she'd appear more genuine if she checked.

"Yes," he said with a nod. "That's right. Two Ls. Okay, here's my number. Once you've stored it, would you call it so I've got your number?"

"Of course." She entered the number he gave her, saved it, then pressed the call button. As the device in his hand began to buzz—he clearly had it on silent mode, which was why the ringing hadn't woken her up earlier—she felt bad all over again. He'd given her the right number, which told her he wasn't just being polite, he genuinely did want to see her again.

And fuck, as much as she kept trying to tell herself it didn't matter... it did. As much as she was trying to stop her brain from going there, it wasn't working.

She liked him. He was smart, handsome, funny, selfless—as evidenced in his chasing of her sunglasses thief—and, if things were different, she'd be jumping at the chance to see him again, to get to know him better. In fact, she could barely reconcile the man she'd spent the last few hours with, with the guy that was about to go and steal thousands, possibly millions, of pounds worth of diamonds from the place up the road. It just didn't compute. However, she'd seen with her own eyes, and heard with her own ears—he was part of the gang, and that was that. Case closed.

"Hey," he said, waving his hand in front of her face. The tiny frown line had appeared between his eyebrows again. "Are you all right? You looked miles away. And you can end the call now—I have your number." He showed her the screen of his phone, still flashing up with an incoming call.

Shaking her head and blinking, she said, "Sorry." She stabbed at the end call button and put her phone in her pocket. "Yeah, I'm fine. Just... hungry, I think. Once you're gone, I think I'll order room service." She forced herself to smile, hoping like hell it looked genuine. "For some reason, I seem to have worked up quite the appetite. Shame you can't stay and sate it with me."

Baxter bit his lip, then pointed at her. "Stop that, woman. Trust me, if I could get out of work tonight, I would. But my hands are tied, and it's important. Now, no more tempting me or making me feel bad, all right? I have to go. Come here." He stuffed his phone into his pocket and reached for her.

She couldn't balk now—doing so might well bring the whole mission crashing down around her ears. *Or is that just what you're telling yourself?*

Closing her eyes in an attempt to hide the anguish that was no doubt projecting from them, she tilted her face up ready to accept his kiss. As if they'd done it a thousand times, they slipped their arms around each other—hers around his neck, his around her waist—and their lips met. The kiss was tender and hot all at once, deepening almost instantly, and Mallory was glad Baxter was holding her so tightly, as her knees felt watery, as though they could give way at any moment.

Her stomach and mind roiled in unison as the two sides of her waged an internal war. It took all of her concentration to keep kissing Baxter. It was important she did—he couldn't be allowed to suspect that something was amiss, particularly at this late stage.

After a minute or so, the strength of her emotions and her attraction to him won out, and she gave everything over to the kiss, hoping to convey to him something she couldn't possibly say: *I'm sorry.*

Eventually, Baxter pulled away, the expression on his face indicating that stopping was the last thing he wanted to do. "Holy fuck," he said, blinking rapidly, "that was some goodbye kiss." He stepped back, then reached down and pressed a hand to his crotch. "I hope that buggers off quickly, or I'm going to get some funny looks from my colleagues!"

She smirked, surprised to find her eyes prickling with the threat of tears. *Fuck. Get him out of here!* "Yeah, you probably would. Least us girls don't have that problem, eh? Let me see you out—I don't want to make you late. Nice to leave things on such a high note, though, huh?"

Baxter nodded and followed her towards the door. "Absolutely. I've no idea how long it'll be before we manage to see each other again, but the memory of that kiss will get me through some lonely nights in the meantime."

Opening the door, she then turned to him and raised her eyebrows. "Hey now, don't ruin it by spinning me a line. You promised, remember?"

Leaning down, he pressed a kiss to her cheek and murmured into her ear, "That wasn't a line." Then he walked past her, out of the room, and down the corridor.

Mallory watched just long enough to see him enter the room next door to the one opposite hers. She closed the door just as the tears started to fall.

Chapter Twelve

Mallory gave herself a few minutes to let it all out. Huddled under the duvet, she sobbed, pounded the pillow and even screamed into it a couple of times, thankful for the hotel's soundproofing.

Then she went to the bathroom and splashed cold water onto her face. Finally, she headed to the mini-bar and retrieved a bottle of icy-cold mineral water. After gulping down half the bottle—part of her wishing it was vodka—she felt able to make the call. She'd known those few minutes wouldn't have made any difference. The thieves weren't meeting until 11pm, giving Mallory and her team several hours to put a plan into place.

Now, those several hours were up, and tension was high. After an extensive briefing with her team—in which Mallory had divulged the intelligence she'd learned from her time with Baxter—they'd all got kitted out in bulletproof vests, and carried guns. They'd received no intelligence to suggest that the group was armed, or even violent, but then, they'd never been caught before. Who knew how they would react when cornered? It just wasn't worth taking the risk. They had the resources, so it made sense to use them.

As she hid inside the darkened Rijksmuseum gift shop—the closest place which afforded a view of the front door of Royal Coster Diamonds—peering through her night-vision binoculars, Mallory's heart pounded. She pulled one sweaty hand from the binoculars and wiped it on her trousers, then the other. Despite having made her decision, her head and heart were still at war. Her head had pointed out that, even if he wasn't caught tonight, which he would be, how on earth could an international diamond scammer, and a spy whose job it was to catch people like him have a relationship? It was like a modern-day version of *Romeo and Juliet,* except without the mushiness and committing suicide.

Her heart, though, was still working hard to convince her that maybe he wasn't that bad of a guy. He didn't hurt people, and if she'd met him under different circumstances, and hadn't known who he was, or what he did for a living, she'd have thought him quite the catch. Gorgeous, smart, funny, a gentleman… he was a damn sight better than the last few idiots she'd dated.

But then, what was the point in having a boyfriend if he was in prison?

She resisted the temptation to punch the plate-glass window

in front of her. She'd come off worst, not to mention confuse the crap out of her colleagues. And it was pointless. All of it was. The angsting, the wondering *what if?* In a few short minutes, Baxter Collinson, along with the rest of the criminal gang, would be caught, rounded up and carted off. And, following any initial questioning, unless she was needed any further in the investigation, she'd be given a few days R&R, then be sent off on her next mission.

Her earpiece crackled into life. "This is alpha one. I've got movement at the rear of the building. Eyes on two targets, closing in on the rear door. Does anyone else see anything?"

Mallory's heart raced faster, and a sudden bout of nausea caused saliva to fill her mouth. Gritting her teeth and swallowing hard, she used the binoculars to scan the street, but saw nothing out of the ordinary. Hardly surprising, though—the front door was on a main road, with a car lane, trams, bicycles… using it would be a risky move in the middle of the night, never mind the relatively early time of 11:10 p.m. But, if she was completely honest with herself, that was precisely why she'd allowed herself to be given this stakeout spot. Normally, if she had a vested interest in a mission, she'd insist on a front row seat for the arrest, even if she wasn't physically involved. But this time, she was happy to sit it out. She just didn't have the stomach to watch the team take Baxter down. And she certainly didn't want to see the look on his face when he realised who she was and what she'd done.

The rest of the team responded with negatives, then she chimed in with, "This is Spider. Negative."

Seconds passed. To Mallory, they felt like hours.

Then, finally, "This is alpha one. I couldn't get close enough to see exactly what they were doing, but somehow they got in without tripping any alarms. Clearly their hacker has been hard at work. One target has entered the building, and two more—no, four more—targets have appeared. All targets are heading inside. Repeat, six targets inside the building. All is quiet so far—I'm going in."

"This is alpha two. Alpha one, I'm following you in. Those at the other entrances, leave one man covering, and the rest fall in for backup."

Oh Christ, this was it. The time for stealth was over. A series of "copy thats" filtered through the comms, then some rapid commands as to who was staying and who was going.

"Spider, are you coming with?" The words didn't come

through her earpiece, but from the man next to her—known as alpha four during operations.

She looked at him blankly. "Me?"

"Yes, Spider, you. This is your collar. Don't you want to be there to see it happen?" He frowned and jerked the barrel of his gun in the direction of the door. "Let's go."

She bit her lip. There was no other option. She was always in the thick of the action, unless a major fire fight was expected, and if she wasn't this time, questions would be asked. Uncomfortable questions that she really didn't want to answer.

Maybe she could figure out a way to be in the room when the arrests took place, but in the background, so she couldn't be seen. She wished she'd worn a helmet and a snood like alpha team, but in the past she'd always refused, insisting that she wanted those she'd hoodwinked to see her, to realise what she'd done, how she'd ruined them. God damn her fucking arrogance! She was paying for it now.

"Copy that, alpha four," she said, the words almost choking her. Luckily, alpha four was too eager to storm the building to notice. They headed out of the museum shop, across the road and around to the rear entrance of Royal Coster Diamonds. Mallory wondered what the hell they'd find when they got there.

They were barely across the threshold when word came. "Confirming, targets have been neutralised. Repeat, targets have been neutralised. They are not armed. We are in the main jewel room. Looks like they were going for a big haul. Marilyn Monroe will be spinning in her grave 'round about now. Send transport ASAP."

A huge part of Mallory wanted to turn and sprint back out of the door. All of her, in fact. But she knew damn well she couldn't. She had to go in there and face up to what she'd done.

Which was what, exactly? Her job? Well, yes, she supposed. But it was more than that. So much more. At some point, what she'd been doing with Baxter had gone way beyond a honey trap, way beyond intelligence gathering, and well into the realms of getting attached. She wasn't far gone enough to think she was falling in love with him—Christ, she'd only known the bloke five minutes—but if circumstances were different, drastically different, then that wasn't an unrealistic thing to happen down the line. Particularly since she sensed that he felt the same. And when he knew the truth, he'd also know she'd betrayed him. He'd want to strangle her, not have sex with her.

In a daze, she hurried after alpha four. Knowing she couldn't run away or put it off, she decided to get it over with. Like ripping a sticking plaster off a cut—the quicker she did it, the sooner the pain would go away and be forgotten about. Though she wasn't convinced the forgetting bit would happen in this situation.

Alpha four burst into the room. She loitered in the corridor, hoping that the low light would hide her identity from anyone that happened to glance in her direction. There was a scuffle as the entire gang was rounded up and handcuffed. A security guard stood off to one side, looking utterly dumbfounded—probably worried about losing his job. Unless he was in on it—in which case the loss of his job would be the least of his worries.

Crackling in her ear. "Transport outside rear entrance, ready when you are, alpha team."

"Copy that."

Bodies began hustling in her direction, and she slammed herself up against the wall of the corridor so hard that she partially winded herself. The usual euphoria she felt at this moment was nowhere to be found. She kept her expression impassive as the criminals were frog-marched past her. Each of them stared at her, probably wondering who the hell she was.

Then someone stared at her that knew *exactly* who she was. Or he thought he did. Holding firm and meeting his gaze, Mallory stuffed her hands casually into her jacket pockets so she could clench her fists without anyone seeing. Her nails bit into her palms so hard that she was sure she'd broken the skin. Pain zipped through her nerve endings, but she didn't wince. She deserved it.

Her pounding heart cracked as she watched Baxter's face go through a myriad of expressions. Recognition, confusion, realisation, shock, anger, then fury. Each emotion as plain as day. Each emotion making her heart crumble that little bit more, until she was sure there was nothing left. Just a void in her chest.

As he got closer, she steeled herself for the inevitable venom that would be spewed in her direction. Insults, name-calling, threats. She'd heard it all in her time, and it had never bothered her before. But this time it was different. Everything was different.

The stony silence she actually got as Baxter was shoved past her was somehow worse. She hadn't been prepared for it, so it cut deeper than any insult could ever have done. Right through to the bone.

Chapter Thirteen

"Spider, you're wanted in the interrogation room," Simon said, peering at Mallory expectantly.

Mallory's stomach lurched. "What? Why?"

He frowned. "I dunno. I'm just the tech guy, remember?"

Despite the turmoil she was in, she rolled her eyes. "You are not *just* the tech guy, Simon. Far from it. But I'm not getting into dishing out compliments right now, okay? Maybe later, when I've found out what's going on."

"All right. I'll be waiting here, for my compliments."

Shaking her head, she headed for the interrogation room, nausea building in her stomach with each subsequent step. She shoved her hands into her pockets to hide the simultaneous sweating and trembling. She didn't know who was in there, but could make an educated guess. Nobody good, that was for sure. In fact, she'd rather walk in there and be faced by a gigantic tarantula than what—or who—she was actually likely to see.

The door was ajar. She pushed it open with her hip, hoping she looked nonchalant as she shoved it closed behind her with her foot. There was only one person in the room, and he was handcuffed to the table.

She knew they were being watched and listened to. Anything that was said or done would be seen, overheard, and scrutinised. All she could do was keep calm and hope nobody realised it had gone beyond faking it for intelligence purposes. But keeping calm in the face of the criminal that had gotten beneath her skin was easier said than done.

Rip off the plaster, Mallory. It's the only way.

Taking a seat opposite Baxter, she forced herself to look him in the eyes. "You wanted to see me, Mr Collinson?"

"So formal all of a sudden, Ms Winchester. Or whatever your real name is."

She shrugged. "Ms Winchester will do. Or Bea. So, what can I do for you?"

Settling back into his chair—as far as his binds would allow, anyway—he smirked. "All right, *Bea*. Since you seem to be so *accommodating,* I'd like to make a deal."

Quirking an eyebrow, she said, "And I'd like to be the next Mrs Brad Pitt. But we don't always get what we want, do we? Life's a bitch." Even as she spoke, though, ideas whirled around her brain. Ways she could get him off the charges, maybe get him a reduced sentence. Or ensure he was in a convenient institution, so she could—

"Cut the crap, Bea. I know perfectly well how this works. I keep my mouth shut, and I'm going to prison for a very long time. Or I can dish the dirt to you guys, give you information you can use. In return I get less time, or end up in some place nicer, maybe with some perks. You're going to have to protect me somehow, anyway, because once the others find out I'm spilling the beans, they'll find a way to get to me. I'll be dead long before I ever get chance to testify. Even if I don't spill the beans, once they realise that I'm the reason—thanks to you, I assume—that we got caught in the first place, I'm dead. Either way, I'm a goner."

Christ, she hadn't thought of it like that. Bad enough that he was going to prison because of her—but if he ended up dead? Her conscience could never handle that.

And nor could her heart.

Another thought occurred to her. Was she allowing her emotions to cloud her judgement? She forced out a snort. "I think perhaps you're being a little melodramatic, Baxter. You and your little gang are thieves and forgers, not cold-blooded killers."

He fixed her with a serious look, making her want to wriggle in her chair. Whether it was with arousal, guilt, or discomfort, she couldn't be sure. "Perhaps, sweet Bea, your team's intelligence isn't quite all it's cracked up to be. I'm the new boy. I've only been working with them for a year. This was only my fourth job—I was still proving myself. And I never did find out what happened to my predecessor. Nothing good, I can guarantee you that. Evan McKellan can be quite the nasty bastard when his back's up against the wall, you know. I've made it a point never to get on the wrong side of him."

Mallory's heart leapt. Only his fourth job? That was something she could definitely use to her... er, *Baxter's* benefit. He wouldn't have so many charges against his name, so his sentence would already be much shorter than the rest of the gang's. But a year with them meant he should still have plenty of valuable information that she and her colleagues could use.

Perhaps things weren't so bad. With luck and planning, she could keep him alive, keep his jail term to an absolute minimum.

Then, when he was out, they could…

She shook her head. What was she thinking? Baxter Collinson wanted a deal in order to save his own—admittedly delicious—arse. He wasn't trying to do her any favours. Chances were he hated her guts for what she'd done to him. He probably never wanted to see her again.

"What are you shaking your head for?"

"Huh?" She snapped her attention back to Baxter, then cleared her throat. "Uh, just thinking, that's all. You're right. Perhaps there are some minor holes in our intelligence. And I'm sure, if you help us to plug those holes, that we can come to a mutually beneficial agreement with regards to what happens to you next."

"So you *are* going to offer me a deal."

She shrugged. "Depends how good you are at plugging holes."

He flashed her one of the wicked grins she'd become so accustomed to, which had the usual effect of making her pussy clench with need. "I think you already know the answer to that. I certainly didn't hear you complaining."

Well aware he was only trying to embarrass her in front of whoever might be listening to their conversation, she refused to give him the satisfaction. Countering his grin with a sickly-sweet smile of her own, she replied, "I graduated from RADA before joining up, you know. With distinction."

His expression didn't falter, but a flicker of… *something*… in his eyes told her that he knew she was lying. And he was pleased about it. "So, what happens now? Are you going to get me this deal, or what?" He smirked. "I'll plug as many holes as you want me to, as often as you like, sweetheart—just as long as you keep me alive."

"For now, *sweetheart,*" she shot back, "you're going into a cell. Don't worry—it'll be away from your buddies, but that's the only perk, I'm afraid. I've got some more interviews to conduct. I'll be back to talk to you again later. Okay, guys, come and get him." She said the last part more loudly, ensuring one of her eavesdropping colleagues would send a pair of officers to come and escort Baxter to a cell.

The seconds before they arrived to take him away were spent in silence. They stared at each other over the table, the atmosphere between them as palpable as ever. Except now, it was tinged with something more than just attraction. Betrayal? Anger? Uncertainty? Probably all of those things, and more besides. Mallory closed her eyes for a moment, reminding herself that she'd done the right thing. Baxter Collinson was a criminal. She'd caught him, and he was now going to be brought to justice. Just because her heart and hormones disagreed with her brain and common sense didn't make it any less true.

Opening her eyes again, she met Baxter's gaze. There, she saw something she hadn't expected. Warmth. Maybe she hadn't blown it with him, after all.

Just then, the door opened and two burly officers came in. They nodded to Mallory. One of them released Baxter from his attachment to the table, then hauled him to his feet. Just before they carted him off, as he drew level with where Mallory had stood from her seat, Baxter said, "Why the hell would you need to marry Brad Pitt, when you can have me?"

Aware she was still being watched and listened to, she didn't react. Inside, though, was a different matter altogether. She simply couldn't get her head around the fact that Baxter didn't hate her for what she'd done. Unless he was just trying to keep her on side, hoping that would encourage her to pull some strings on his behalf. That was a definite possibility.

"See you later, Mr Collinson," she said dispassionately, then followed the three men out into the corridor. She waited until they were out of sight—not wanting Baxter to know she'd been lying about the other interviews—then turned in the opposite direction to where they'd gone and headed for the room her boss was temporarily using as an office.

She tapped on the door.

"Come in!" came the response.

Wesley Holt, codename Hummingbird, was an incredibly astute man. He certainly wouldn't have gotten to his position if he wasn't. It was possible that he'd work out her real feelings in an instant. So it was with a considerable amount of nerves that Mallory entered the room. She gave a polite smile, then turned and closed the door behind her. "Hello, sir."

Wesley returned her smile and indicated the seat on her side of the desk. "Hello, Spider. Come to report in?"

Taking the seat, she replied, "Yes, sir. A preliminary report, anyway. I'm hoping that by the end of the day we will have a much bigger picture of just what's been going on with this gang. I've just finished speaking with Baxter Collinson."

"Ah, yes. Your pet diamond thief. Got plenty to say, has he?"

Mallory's heart missed a beat. *Pet diamond thief?* What the hell did he mean by that? She gulped and quickly nodded, hoping that he wouldn't notice her panic. "Oh yes," she replied, her tone calm and collected—everything she wasn't on the inside. "He's ready to sing like the proverbial canary. But he's smart, sir—he won't talk just for the sake of it, or because he feels it's the right thing to do. He's self-serving. Wants a deal of some kind. Which is something I'm hoping you can advise me on."

"Certainly, Spider. I'm sure we can sort something out. First, though, give me your report."

"Of course, sir." She pointed to the carafe of water between them on the desk. "Do you mind?"

"Not at all. Pour two glasses, please."

She did as she was told, then settled back into her seat and downed half the glass of water. Then she put it on the desk and launched in to her verbal report.

A good while later and she was done. Her mouth and throat dry from all the talking, she finished the rest of the water as she waited for Wesley's response.

"So, all in all, an incredibly successful mission. We'd been prepared for the long game, so the fact it all happened so quickly might have had us somewhat on the back foot to begin with, but mainly thanks to you, Spider, we achieved our goal with the minimum of fuss. Excellent. Just superb. Couldn't have wished for a better result." Wesley picked up his own glass and took a drink. "So... about Collinson. From what you've told me about him, he sounds like a smart boy."

Ensuring she kept her tone neutral, she replied, "Yes, sir. It's probably what led the gang to recruit him in the first place. He's intelligent, articulate and discreet—with the exception of the phone call I overheard, of course. He might be smart, but that was an incredibly stupid move."

Wesley shrugged. "It was, but he wasn't to know who you were. He didn't even know you were awake."

"No, he wasn't, and he didn't. But it was still idiotic. He should never been on that call while he was in the same room as me."

"Correct—he shouldn't have. But he's a thief, not an espionage operative. He can learn."

"Excuse me?" Mallory frowned. *Learn what?*

Wesley sighed and sat back in his seat, staring into the middle distance. He was a handsome man in his late fifties, with rapidly greying hair and piercing blue eyes that seemed to see right through everyone they peered at. Although he scared her more than a little, she also liked him. And she respected him a hell of a lot. That, and the fact he was her boss, stopped her from prompting him when he remained silent. He'd speak when he was ready. What bothered her was the *reason* behind his delay. Undoubtedly he knew exactly what he was going to say, but was finding it difficult to get the words out.

What the hell is going on?

Almost a minute passed before Wesley opened his mouth. He cleared his throat, then leaned forward and placed his elbows on the desk. Steepling his fingers, he rested his chin on them and fixed Mallory in his penetrating gaze. "You're not going to like this, Spider, I'm afraid."

The sick feeling in her stomach had abated as she'd given her report, but now returned with a vengeance. "Sir..?"

"Like you said, Collinson is smart. And since this operation began, some fresh information came to light, something that I'm only sharing with you now because it's pertinent. Baxter Collinson is known to us in a capacity other than thief—or should I say *was*. Turns out my predecessor tried to recruit him when he was at Cambridge. Obviously, he failed. No idea why—or how Collinson then ended up getting into a life of crime. I'm sure that will all come to light soon enough. But, all things considered, I think now is a good time to get him on board. See if we can't change his mind, as his back's up against the wall. Provided we can mould him the way we want to, I believe he'll be a good asset."

Mallory's mouth dropped open. She stared at Wesley, uncomprehending. Several seconds passed with her thoughts whirling around her head in an alarming manner, none of them making any sense.

Finally, when she could take it no more, she burst out, "You want to *recruit* him? Sir," she added, remembering her place at the very last second.

"Yes. I did warn you that you weren't going to like it. And I believe you'll like this even less..."

Stifling a groan, Mallory said tentatively, "Sir..?"

"I want *you* to recruit him. He wants a deal—so offer him this one. With the proviso that he passes the training—and we'll be hard on him, though no need to tell him that part—he comes to work for us, and this... *incident* will be wiped off his record permanently. It'll be like it never happened. He will, of course, also have to surrender any of his remaining ill-gotten gains from previous jobs with the gang. As a gesture of goodwill and commitment."

Mallory didn't know whether to laugh, cry, scream, or dance around the room. But she couldn't do any of those things. Letting Wesley Holt know that recruiting Baxter Collinson was the answer to all of her problems would be a huge mistake. Romantic—or even just sexual—entanglements between fellow operatives were severely frowned upon, and if Wesley found out that there was more between her and Baxter than some mission-necessary shagging, he'd withdraw the offer in the blink of an eye.

Unwilling to let this incredible chance slip between her—or Baxter's—fingers, she nodded, hoping that Wesley would assume her hesitation was down to Baxter's criminal status. "Yes, sir. Of course, sir. For what it's worth, in my relatively limited knowledge of the man, I don't think he'll take much persuading."

"No, nor do I, Spider. Do you want to go and give him the good news?"

Mallory got to her feet. "Yes, sir, of course. Will there be anything else?" She took a step towards the door.

"Actually, yes—I forgot. If Collinson *does* accept the offer, I want you to be the one to take charge of his training, and to be his mentor. I'll leave it with you as to whether you let him in on that particular piece of information. He's probably not your biggest fan right now, so that might influence his decision."

She gave a curt nod. "Of course, sir. I'll go and see him right away and let you know what happens."

"Very good. Thank you, Spider."

"Thank you, sir." With that, she turned on her heel and strode to the door.

It was only when she was safely locked into a cubicle in the ladies' toilets that she let the full consequences of what was happening sink in.

Chapter Fourteen

Two weeks later

Mallory groaned. How could she *possibly* have thought this was the answer to all of her problems?

Sequestered in one of the section's central London facilities, she and Baxter were training. In their line of work, *training* actually covered many, many bases. As a covert government department which didn't fit into a neat little box, and with minimal personnel, they had to be versatile. At some point, she guessed, Baxter would be sent to an assessment centre for psychometric aptitude tests and vetting—stuff she couldn't possibly do. Nor would she want to. And surely they'd have to bend the rules in terms of vetting—wouldn't being an ex-criminal immediately raise red flags, otherwise? Following that, he'd then be sent to a military base on the south coast to work on decision making, problem solving, working alone and as part of a team, identifying targets, surveillance, counter-surveillance, communications, dead-letter drops, agent handling, personal security, cover stories and much more.

Wesley hadn't said as much, but she suspected the idea was that she got to decide whether Baxter was even suitable to be sent to the assessment centre and then the base. If she didn't believe he was good enough, or simply wasn't right for the job, then they'd save much-needed funds by not sending him for needless training off-site.

So for now, they were sticking with the relatively simple stuff, which Mallory *could* help out with. They were currently working out—their physical fitness and abilities were just as important as their mental ones. She herself hit the gym, went running or sparred with one of her colleagues every opportunity she got—not always possible when on a mission, but otherwise, a high priority—but whether a Cambridge-educated diamond thief could keep up with her remained to be seen. If he couldn't, then he'd be kicked out. What would happen to him then, she had no idea.

Would Wesley withdraw the offer and leave him open to the mercy of the legal system and possible retribution from the rest of the gang? They'd definitely want to get their revenge, particularly since Baxter had, by now, told her section everything he knew, allowing them to put his ex-buddies in prison for a very long time.

She couldn't worry about the future too much, however. Her present was doing a damn good job of getting her riled up as it was.

Even with headphones in, workout music blaring, and her going hell for leather on the treadmill, she was still incredibly aware of Baxter's every move on the cross-trainer he'd hopped onto after a quick warm up. The mirrors on each wall of the compact but well-equipped gym meant there was no getting away from him—not unless she closed her eyes. And given she didn't want to end up face-planting the machine, or tumbling right off it, that wasn't an option.

Therefore, she was forced to endure the sight of Baxter, in his tight white T-shirt and black shorts, getting all hot and sweaty, his muscles tensing and flexing. As a result of the pleasing view, she was also enduring epic shag flashbacks, as Bridget Jones would say. She groaned again, safe in the knowledge that he, too, had music pumping through headphones and couldn't hear her.

This was ridiculous. What she had originally thought was a good thing—i.e., him being recruited rather than thrown in prison and possibly killed—was now torture. When she'd slept with him, it had been part of her job and therefore perfectly okay in the eyes of the powers that be. Now, however, they were colleagues and suddenly, what had been perfectly okay—even encouraged—was completely out of the question. She must have been insane to think that they could simply pick up where they'd left off. Maybe it was the speed at which things had happened that had scrambled her brain—there had been approximately thirty-two hours between her setting eyes on Baxter for the first time and having him arrested.

It wouldn't be so bad if she didn't have to see him, day in, day out. After all, before the bust, they'd barely known each other. Yes, she'd become fond of him and had most definitely had the hots for him, but that would have faded. Out of sight, out of mind. But since she'd been appointed his mentor, he was constantly in sight, and therefore, constantly in mind.

For the last two weeks, she'd spent almost every working minute with him. As an agent, he was shaping up incredibly well, and she was already fairly certain he'd pass any test or assessment he was given. And as a person, he was the attractive, funny, smart man she'd briefly come to know, and she really wished he wasn't. Yes, he was an ex-criminal, and he said stupid things at times, but he appealed to her on every level. It was a huge struggle to keep him at arm's length when what she really wanted to do was pounce on him and for them to screw each other's brains out.

The only saving grace was that he seemed to understand why she'd gone from being happy to share lunch, champagne, luxury chocolates and a bed with him, to a consummate professional. Or she assumed he understood. They hadn't talked about it, hadn't even mentioned what had happened between them since he'd made the comment about having him instead of Brad Pitt. Clearly, staying out of prison and having his slate wiped clean was more important—and who could blame him?

Mallory pressed the button on her treadmill to increase the speed—hoping the additional physical exertion would take her mind off Baxter.

For a while, it worked. She pounded away on the machine, giving it her all, until so much sweat poured from her that it started to sting her eyes, and her entire body ached. She slowed the speed in increments until she was at a walking pace, then carefully stepped off, swiping at her forehead with the back of her hand.

Just then, a smiling Baxter appeared beside her, his headphones dangling around his neck. She removed her own. "You need something, Collinson?" she asked, wincing internally as she realised just how harshly her words had come out.

His smile dimmed briefly, but quickly bounced back. "I wondered if you'd be able to spot me on the bench? No problem if not—I can do something else."

"No, no," she said brightly in an attempt to assuage her guilt somewhat, "that's fine—I can do that. Lead the way." *Yeah, Mallory, what a great idea—get up close and personal with the guy while he lifts weights. That's really going to help you forget how much you'd like to get him naked, isn't it?*

She followed Baxter over to the weight bench, then stepped into position behind it. Baxter was just about to lie down when the door opened and Zoe Rangemore, a member of the support team, came in. "Scott; Collinson—you're wanted in the boss's office."

Mallory frowned. "Any idea what for, Rangemore?"

The pretty brunette shook her head. "'Fraid not. Wesley didn't give any details, just that he wanted you two in there, pronto."

"Pronto as in covered in sweat and stinking to high heaven?"

Rangemore nodded. "As in, immediately."

"Okay, we're on our way. Come on, Collinson." Mallory strode from the room without waiting to see if he was following. A cold sensation swirled in her gut. What the hell could this be about?

Although she was glad she and her errant hormones had been saved from a close up of Baxter and his pumping muscles, she wondered if somehow the powers that be had figured out there was something between the two of them. But how was that even possible? Because other than inside her head, there *wasn't* anything between the two of them, not since the moment he'd walked out of her hotel room in Amsterdam.

As soon as her brain had clicked into gear and she'd realised just how his recruitment to the section changed things, she'd been the very epitome of professional. No lingering glances, no flirting, no joking around—hell, she barely even conversed with him other than the essentials to get them through the day. She was like a bloody robot. A new-boy-training, bad-guy-catching robot. Except she hadn't gotten so much as a whiff of a bad guy since taking down Baxter and his gang. She'd been ordered to focus solely on training and mentoring him, despite the fact there were still bad people out there that needed taking down. She knew Baxter was a special case, but they had dedicated teams for training new recruits—why had the task fallen to her?

She narrowed her eyes as a thought occurred to her. Had Wesley and the other higher-ups done it on purpose? Thrown the two of them together on a daily basis to see if they could be in close proximity without succumbing to lust? Was this a fucking *test*?

She pulled herself together as rapid footsteps approached and Baxter fell into step beside her. "Bloody hell, B-Mallory, I know Rangemore said immediately, but you left that room like a bat out of hell! What do you reckon this is all about? I'm doing all right, aren't I? I'm not in trouble?"

Resolutely ignoring that he had, once again, slipped up and almost called her Bea, she shook her head. "It's never a good idea to keep the boss waiting. As for what this is about, I've been wondering the same thing myself. And no, I don't think you're in trouble. You've been doing just fine."

In truth, he'd been doing more than *just fine,* but it wasn't her job to massage his ego. She'd much rather massage his—

She stopped the thought before it was fully formed, thanking her lucky stars when they reached Wesley's office. Out of habit, she glanced down to make sure she was presentable, then remembered it was pointless. They'd been commanded to the office straight from the gym, so the boss could hardly complain if they looked like shit and smelled worse.

Rolling her eyes, she knocked on the door.

"Come in!"

Baxter, ever the gentleman, gestured she should go first. Or was he sacrificing her by allowing her into the lion's den ahead of him? It didn't matter either way. She opened the door and crossed the threshold, letting the momentum carry her right up to Wesley's desk. He sat behind it in his usual spot, looking perfectly calm and collected. But that didn't necessarily mean anything. He was a spymaster, after all. "You wanted to see us, sir?"

"Yes," he replied with a curt nod. "Close the door, Collinson. Sit down, both of you."

Wesley started speaking as soon as the door was closed, not even waiting for Baxter to take his seat. "I'm sorry I had to drag you away from your training session, but this is urgent. We've just had word that someone on our radar has upped their game. This lowlife," he tapped the screen of his iPad a couple of times, then slid it across the desk to them so they could see the photograph he'd pulled up, "has been passing secrets on to the Russians for a while. Just small fry up until now, nothing worth acting on. But the latest update is that his contact is trying to find out some things that we *really* don't want the Russians to know. Don't want *anyone* to know. Things that could put the country's whole defence strategy and framework at risk. Needless to say, we have to stop this from happening. The Russians can *not* get their hands on that intelligence."

"Of course, sir," Mallory said, studying the image on the screen. The man pictured was Caucasian, with dark hair and eyes, in his mid-to-late forties and was fairly overweight. She doubted very much he was a physical threat, but one should never underestimate a person. "What do you need me to do?"

Wesley raised his eyebrows and looked from Mallory to Baxter, and back again. "I need *both of you* to track him down, find out who he's liaising with and then call in a team to grab them both before any sensitive information is released. Alternatively, if the opportunity presents itself, you should find out who the Russian liaison is working for."

"Track him down, sir?" She deliberately didn't say anything about the fact he wanted Baxter to go along too. Making an issue of it might just unintentionally show her hand.

"Yes." Wesley ran his hands through his hair and released a

huff of frustration. "As you know, Spider, we are good, but we are not infallible. Like I said, everything passing through this target has been small fry up until now, so we haven't seen the need to allocate anything other than minimal resources to him. But red flags started going up just a couple of hours ago, and by the time we realised what he was up to, he was boarding a plane out of Heathrow."

"To where, sir?" she asked.

"Romania. He's flying into Bucharest airport. Where he's headed from there I'm not sure, but will update you as and when I have more information. I need you two on the next flight out. Go and shower and get anything you'll need for a few nights away, then come back. By that time I'll have a full briefing pack available for you." He paused, then slid his gaze over to Baxter, assessing him coolly. "You've been awfully quiet, Collinson. Are you up for this?"

Baxter nodded. "Yes, sir, absolutely! I just… wasn't expecting it, that's all. I thought I was only in training mode right now."

Narrowing his eyes, Wesley replied, "You are *still* in training mode. Are we clear? You are to do absolutely everything that Spider tells you to do. You follow her lead, follow her commands, *everything*. It's unlikely you'll have to engage—as soon as I'm done with you two I'm going to get on the phone and make sure we've got a team to take them down as soon as we have enough evidence to ensure we can hold them without complaint. Understand? This is an intelligence-gathering mission only."

In unison, she and Baxter replied, "Yes, sir."

"Good. Now get a move on. If the Russians get their hands on that information, we're all fucked."

She and Baxter left the office in silence and made their way to the locker rooms. As she pushed the door into the ladies' area, she threw over her shoulder, "Meet you out here in fifteen."

"Copy that."

Only when she'd crossed the threshold did she allow herself a small smile. He was getting the hang of the language they used, but the mission they were being sent on was something else entirely. She'd be fine, naturally, but Baxter was being thrown in at the deep end. What she couldn't understand was *why* they were being sent. Yes, they were a small team, but they were big enough to have someone spare to go and follow this Russian-loving, loose-lipped arsehole, surely? And if they were so tight on resources, why were they using her to babysit the new boy, instead of following all the usual protocols?

She stripped off her workout gear and dove into the shower, questions filling her brain quicker than she could answer them.

One thing was for sure, though.

If this was a test, it was one she fully intended to pass.

Chapter Fifteen

As yet more people crammed into the Tube car at Leicester Square, forcing Mallory and Baxter to squeeze even further into the corner they'd snagged, he asked, "Why, exactly, are we getting the Tube instead of a taxi? Or a lift?"

Trying hard to ignore what Baxter's *very* close proximity was doing to her, she rolled her eyes and replied, "Because it's quicker. At this time of day it'd take forever just to get out of central London in a car, never mind all the way to Heathrow. And, if you remember, time is of the essence." Since their incredibly public location meant she couldn't elaborate, she settled for giving him a hard stare.

Annoyingly, his response was a wide grin. "Yes it is, isn't it? Must hurry, so we don't miss our flight."

His delighted expression made him look more like an excited traveller than a trainee spy going on his first mission, but she grudgingly admitted to herself that that was a good thing. The less they both looked and acted like government operatives, the better. Perhaps that was why Wesley had sent them both—so they could act like a couple, or at the very least, good friends holidaying together. A lone woman would stand out much more, and might attract unwanted attention from lecherous males. Granted, she was very adept at dealing with those kinds of situations, but it was better she didn't draw any attention to herself in the first place—of the lecherous male variety or otherwise.

Once they got out of zone one, the number of passengers gradually reduced, but because many of the replacement passengers that boarded were carrying luggage, also bound for the airport, the car was no less crowded. But at least the luggage didn't have body odour.

The overall journey time might be just a few minutes shy of an hour, but to Mallory, it felt like forever. She had been squished up against the door at the end of the car for some time, with Baxter in front of her, shielding her from everyone else. Whether that was intentional or not, she wasn't sure. Either way she wasn't going to protest—he'd saved her from being pushed and jostled, potentially groped, and he smelled nice. The combination of his freshly-showered body and hair, and whatever cologne he'd splashed on had been quite the treat compared to the usual London Underground aroma of stale sweat, bad breath and hot, humid air. But while the shielding and the pleasant smell was amazing, the fact it was *Baxter* doing the shielding and the smelling nice proved incredibly problematic.

As a result, she and her tortured hormones were ecstatic when the train finally pulled in at their destination. They headed for the doors—their backpacks making it relatively easy to move through the car and out onto the platform, compared to the travellers lugging large and heavy suitcases around. Their light load also meant they'd be able to get off the plane in Bucharest, go through passport control, and get out of the airport quickly, without having to hang around at the carousel waiting for luggage.

As she'd expected, their check-in and airport security checks went without a hitch, and soon they were ensconced in one of the VIP lounges—one of the few perks of the job. The main reason they had access was because their targets often did. In this case, of course, their target was already long gone—though he might have been in this exact area several hours previously. But it also came in handy because there were fewer people around, allowing them a little more privacy in order to check out the briefing materials and discuss their action plan.

Mallory had just pulled out her tablet when Baxter stood and said, "Is it all right if I leave my bag here? I'm just going to use the facilities then grab a drink. You want one?"

"Yes, that's fine—I'll watch it. And a coffee would be great—thanks."

He gave a quick nod before turning and walking in the direction of the toilets. She watched him go, glad to be away from him even for just a few minutes, but at the same time enjoying the view of his delectable arse and long legs in the snug jeans. She closed her eyes and shook her head quickly, trying to rattle him right out of her brain so she could focus her attention on the briefing information. Lusting after her unattainable new colleague was certainly not going to help with that.

She opened her eyes again, opened the relevant file on the device and began reading.

By the time Baxter came back, she'd finished. She flashed him a smile and took the proffered coffee with one hand, while passing him the tablet with the other. "Thank you. Here. Read this."

It wasn't necessary for him to read it, since he was only there to do everything she told him, but it was a good way for him to learn. More importantly, she was eager to keep him occupied. This was the first time they'd been alone together outside of the section's building since Amsterdam. The first time they'd been away from prying eyes and walls with ears. He might have known better than to bring up what had happened between them when there was a chance of being overheard, but now there was no reason to keep quiet. And the last thing she wanted to do was talk—about that particular topic, anyway.

Her phone vibrated, and she swapped her coffee to her other hand so she could retrieve the device from her pocket. A text message from HQ.

Have a lovely time in Brasov. You just missed the 16.03 train, so you might as well hire a car. We have a friend in the area you can stay with.

She quickly decoded the message in her head. Their target—a man by the name of Thomas Hollis—had just gotten on the 16.03 train to Brasov, and that there was someone in Brasov that could keep an eye on him and feed information back to them until they got there.

All right, so Brasov it was. Sending a quick response to confirm receipt of the message, she navigated to the browser and typed in the name of their destination and started digging up all the information she needed to be prepared for the trip. She'd been to Bucharest before—for work, not pleasure—but never anywhere else in the country, so the more she knew upfront, the better. It would save time once they arrived.

"Bea?" The use of her current alias—Baxter hadn't mentioned her fake name to his gang, so there'd been no reason to retire it—spoken in such a serious tone, made her heart sink. God, this was it. They still had about an hour before they needed to head for their departure gate, so other than the ladies', she really had nowhere to hide, no way of avoiding the conversation. *Shit.*

In a delaying tactic even she knew was ridiculous, she put her phone back in her pocket before responding. "Yes?" she replied, hoping the bored tone and expression she'd adopted would deter him.

He handed her the tablet. "All done. So, what's the plan?"

She gaped at him for a moment, then hurriedly got a grip. Thankful that she appeared to have dodged a bullet, she looked around to make sure no one was nearby that might hear their conversation. Not that she was about to say anything that would sound odd for a traveller, but in their job, there was no such thing as too careful. "Fly to Bucharest, hire a car, get hold of a map, then hit the road. Head to Transylvania."

"*Transylvania?*" Baxter's voice was quiet, but there was no mistaking his incredulity.

She couldn't help laughing, especially at his expression. He looked as though someone had just walked past him, completely naked. "Yes, why? Do you have an aversion to Transylvania?"

He frowned. "No… I… I've never been, I just—"

"Thought it was full of vampires?"

"No…" He took a sip of his coffee, his expression now sullen as a result of her teasing.

"Then what's the problem?"

"I dunno. I just thought we'd be…" Subtly, he checked around them. Once he was satisfied, he continued, "Staying in the capital city—Bucharest, isn't it? So our, er, *hotel* is in Transylvania, is it? Why's that?"

Easily picking up on what he actually meant by *hotel,* she replied, "Bucharest is too busy. Too many people around. Eyes watching, ears listening." She leaned in close to him, playing the part of adoring lover and hoping he took her cue. "There's more *privacy* in the mountains."

Giving her an indulgent smile and pressing a kiss to her hair—a move which felt far too natural for her liking—he said, "Oh, I like the sound of that. *Privacy.* So whereabouts are we going? My knowledge of that area is non-existent, but I'm guessing that Transylvania is a little bit bigger than Regent's Park?"

She mirrored his smile, wishing her heart would stop racing. *Stupid bloody heart. I don't want you involved in this, so bugger off.* "Just a little bit, babe. It's even bigger than Richmond Park. Around 100,000 square metres. We're going to a city called Brasov, in the south east. It'll be about a three hour drive from the airport, all being well."

"Okay then. Sounds great. Bring on the plane!"

There was nothing more to share for the time being, with or without using code words and innuendo, so she switched off the tablet and put it away in her bag, then retrieved her Kindle. If she feigned interest in a book, perhaps he'd take the hint and leave her in peace for a while. She wasn't holding out much hope that he'd keep quiet in the run up to boarding and then for the entire three hour and ten minute flight, but any time at all where he didn't try to engage her in an awkward conversation was a bonus.

After around ten minutes, she gave up. She'd been staring at the same page on her screen and, despite the author being one of her favourites, hadn't taken in a single word. She carefully turned her attention to Baxter in her peripheral vision. He'd taken the hint all right, and had retrieved a tablet of his own. He, however, wasn't reading—or attempting to read, anyway. Figuring he was absorbed enough in his game not to notice what she was doing, she turned her head to look at what he was playing. She smirked as she recognised the fun but bonkers strategy game where you used plants to kill zombie invaders in your garden.

She sneaked a peek at his face. He looked young, almost child-like, as his wide eyes took in the action and reacted to it with a series of rapid taps on the screen and a bunch of muttering littered with the occasional expletive. It was a side to him she hadn't yet seen, and she kinda liked it.

On the flip side, though, it reminded her he was human. Stifling a groan, she looked in the opposite direction and sat back heavily in her chair. Maybe she was going about this all wrong. Maybe avoiding the topic was the worst thing she could do. If they just talked about it, got everything out in the open, they could remind themselves why their current situation meant they couldn't possibly be any more than colleagues, then move on and continue with their jobs and lives.

Baxter wasn't an idiot—he'd understand. He was also a decent guy—recent criminal past notwithstanding—and she owed him a conversation, at least.

Getting to her feet, she wandered slowly over to the nearest departures information board and scanned it for their flight details. Just as she spotted it, the listing changed and a gate number came up. *Thank God for that!* A distraction.

She turned and made her way back over to Baxter, a wide smile on her face. In spite of her outward appearance, though, a heavy weight sat in her stomach. She was well aware of what a coward she was being, and she didn't like it. It was a new experience for her. Normally she faced things head on, dealt with them, and moved on.

Why the hell were things so different this time? What was it about Baxter Collinson that had turned her from her usual ballsy self into someone that would do anything to avoid an uncomfortable situation?

Chapter Sixteen

"In a strange twist of fate," Baxter said, glancing over at Mallory as she drove the car out of the airport complex, "I'm now reversing my question of earlier and asking why we're driving, instead of getting the train. Didn't you say Hollis caught the train to Brasov?"

Mallory allowed herself a small smile. He still had a hell of a lot to learn. "Yes, he did. And if we'd been closer behind him and able to catch the *same* train, then that's what we'd have done. But since he's a good few hours in front of us, there's no point. This way, we go straight there, are involved with less people along the way, and, more importantly, the car means we're instantly mobile once we get there."

From the corner of her eye, she saw him nod. "Fair enough. So," he lifted the map that had been resting across his knees, "I guess I'm navigating, huh?"

"Not exactly. I've got a navigation app on my phone. You're the backup in case I lose signal, or the battery dies or something."

"Wow. You really do think of everything."

He sounded genuinely impressed, and she briefly turned her head to look at him before responding with a shrug, "It's my job to think of everything. To be prepared. A bit like a Girl Scout, I suppose. Except it's more dangerous, exciting and important."

Baxter remained silent as she navigated out onto the main road. Once safely in a traffic lane and trundling along, she retrieved her phone and held it out to him. "Could you sort out the sat-nav, please? I knew I had to go north on this road, and that we stay on here for a while, but after that I'm stuck."

Taking the phone, he replied, "Sure," and set about pulling up the relevant app. "So am I just putting in Brasov, or do you have a specific address?"

"No, not yet. Just Brasov is fine, thanks."

"No problem." He set up the route planner, then carefully placed the phone on the magnetic holder mounted to the vehicle's dashboard. Then he fell silent once more.

Mallory fidgeted in her seat, keeping her eyes firmly on the road. She hadn't spent a great deal of time in Romania, but if her visit to Bucharest a couple of years ago was anything to go by, the drivers were insane. And there were a *lot* of them. Fortunately here, on the road heading away from the capital city, the traffic wasn't too bad and flowed well. But she still didn't want to risk being blindsided by an inconsiderate twat who had no idea that the UK's national security was currently dependent on her.

As though he'd read her mind, Baxter suddenly spoke. "It *is* important, isn't it?" His voice was quiet, thoughtful, and she frowned.

"What?"

"Your job. You said it's dangerous, exciting and *important.* I knew all of that, of course, in some way. But it didn't really sink in until now. All the training and exercises are necessary, I know, but I guess they've made it all feel like it's not real, that we're just playing spy games. Maybe I've just been in a daze, I don't know, but suddenly now it's hit me that we're actually out in the field, chasing after someone who could endanger our country. And if we don't stop him…well, who knows what could happen?"

Well, that certainly explains why he's been so quiet. She felt stupid all of a sudden. All she'd been worrying about for the past few hours was him broaching the topic of the two of them. But Baxter actually had *way* more important things on his mind—and rightly so. Why the hell did two tiny, insignificant people matter when a whole country's safety was at risk? She berated herself for her sheer arrogance. It would serve her right if something went amiss now—she'd been so far up her own arse that she hadn't been giving the job one hundred per cent of her attention. Well, that was about to change.

"We *will* stop him. Emphasis on *we.* Because it's not just *my* job, Baxter. It's yours now, too."

"Only if I pass whatever tests or assessments I'm given."

"Officially speaking, yes. But right now, you're working. You're a part of this operation, so its success depends on you as well as me."

"No pressure, then!"

She chuckled. "You're going to have to get used to pressure if you're serious about this. It's *all about* pressure. Granted, some missions—like my last one, for example—aren't about life and death, but they're still important. For the most part, though, they're about stopping seriously bad people doing seriously bad things."

"So how did you end up on your last mission? It sounds a bit… tame compared to the stuff you usually do. Not that I know what you usually do, but you just used the phrase 'life and death' and that also applies to what we're doing right now. Diamond thieves are small fry in comparison."

"Honestly—I have no idea. It probably doesn't seem like that on TV and in films, but I genuinely just go where I'm told and take down who I'm told to take down. The…" she paused to think of a suitable description for it, then decided to keep it simple, "Amsterdam job was a little different to my usual, but it was fine. I handled it."

"You certainly did," he replied darkly.

Glancing over and clocking his sullen expression, she spluttered out a laugh. "What? You can't seriously hold it against me? One; I was doing my job, and two; you were breaking the law—multiple laws, actually—to the tune of millions of pounds. What was I supposed to do—slap you on the wrist, then tell you not to do it again and to run along now?"

"No, of course not. I'm just…" He blew out a breath. "I guess I'm having trouble adjusting. It's all happened so fast. One minute I was part of a slick operation and earning the sort of money most people only ever dream of, and now—"

"You're part of another slick operation where you're currently not being paid anything at all, and if you pass the probationary period, you'll be earning reasonable money, but not nearly enough considering you put your life on the line on a regular basis?" she finished for him.

He snorted. "Yeah, something like that. But I'm guessing you don't do it for the money. It's all about the glory."

She gave him an incredulous look. "The *glory?* What glory? Yes, I take down some incredibly evil motherfuckers, but I can't *tell* anyone about it! I don't get my name in newspapers or on TV. My own parents think I'm a bloody advertising sales executive. Not exactly heroic! All I get is the occasional 'well done' or 'good job' from Wesley. That's it."

"But you must get a sense of achievement in yourself? I have no idea what you've done in the past, but let's just say you're responsible for shutting down a terrorist operation, or thwarting a terror plot. Surely that's an amazing feeling?"

"Well… yeah. But I wouldn't call it glory. More like job satisfaction. I do it for that, and to keep people safe, and to remove others from harm. It's as simple as that." She smiled as a thought occurred to her. "Don't get me wrong, though, if Wesley offered me a humungous pay rise, I'd snatch his hand off!"

Baxter chuckled. "Glad to see there's a normal person underneath all that righteousness."

A flash of irritation passed through her. "Doing what I do to keep people—and our country—safe doesn't make me righteous. I'm not a bloody angel. I have to do some very unpleasant, deceitful things in my line of work. I have to lie, and pretend, and earn people's trust—you of all people should know that."

As soon as the words were out of her mouth, she wanted to kick herself. After all that, she'd been the one to bring it up. For fuck's sake!

There was a brief pause, then Baxter asked quietly, "So it was all lies, was it? All pretend? And I was just the idiot who fell for it."

Heat prickled all over Mallory's skin. "I'm driving, Baxter. I don't think this is the best time to be discussing this. I need to concentrate."

"No. Of course, you're right. Besides, I want to be able to look you in the eyes when we *do* have the discussion. And we *will* have it—mark my words."

His words and tone were bossy, bombastic, and made her itch to slap his gorgeous face. But she couldn't bring herself to argue with him—mainly because, much as she'd been desperate to avoid it, the discussion needed to be had. Then they could move on. All she had to do was keep her focus on the moving on part, the *after* part, and that would help to get her through the no doubt excruciating bit in the middle. "Fine. But for now, let's change the subject. Please?"

"Yes. All right."

Silence reigned once more, and Mallory turned her attention to the app on her phone, to see how much further they had to go. *Ugh—that far, still?* She stifled a groan. Christ—she was beginning to have her doubts that her sanity would survive the car journey, never mind the rest of the mission.

She shook her head, once more feeling the urge to slap Baxter. He was trouble with a capital T—to her body *and* her mind—and she was stuck with him for the next couple of days. Maybe this was her punishment; she didn't believe in God, but she *did* believe in karma—so perhaps this was it. The payback for...

She stopped herself mid-thought. What exactly *had* she

done?

Her job, she reminded herself. She'd done her job. What was so wrong in that?

Several more miles passed, the only sounds being the gentle purr of the engine, and the rumble of the tyres on the road surface, punctuated by the occasional horn honking as the Romanian drivers pissed each other off. She couldn't decide if there were more suicidal motorists or homicidal ones. Either way, she'd be glad to get to Brasov.

The relative peace lulled her into a more relaxed state, and she allowed her mind to wander.

But that turned out to be the worst possible thing she could have done. Because, no sooner had she internally asked herself the question again—*what was so wrong in doing my job?*—than her brain supplied the answer. The true, real, unhindered and uncensored answer—*there's nothing wrong with you doing your job, Mallory. It's the fact that you started to fall for your target in the process that's the problem. The target who is now your colleague.* A maniacal laugh echoed around the inside of her head. *You are so fucking screwed.*

Well, that was her sanity officially gone, then.

Blissfully unaware of what was going on inside Mallory's increasingly nutty brain, Baxter suddenly piped up, "Oh, Bran Castle!"

Frowning, she glanced over at him. "What?" she snapped. "What the hell are you talking about?"

"No need to get snippy with me. You're the one that wanted to change the bloody subject. I just spotted Bran Castle on the map, that's all. It's not far from Brasov—I had no idea."

"So what?"

She'd turned her attention back to the road, but in her peripheral vision she saw him shake his head. "I thought you were supposed to be smart. Bran Castle is perhaps better known as Dracula's Castle—i.e. the place Bram Stoker made famous by setting his novel there, despite having never been. It's a shame we're only *posing* as tourists, as that would be an amazing place to go and visit." He let out a melodramatic sigh. "Still, I *suppose* finding and apprehending a man on the verge of selling secrets to another country and endangering our very existence is more important."

The laugh escaped before she could stop it. She'd been so

caught up in her stupid angst that she'd forgotten just how funny he was. Playing along, she replied, "Yeah, I *suppose* you're right. Maybe we can go there later, eh? After we've caught the bad guy."

"Later," Baxter agreed jovially.

The funniest part was, she actually thought she meant it.

Chapter Seventeen

After checking in at their hotel in the centre of Brasov—HQ had luckily managed to get them into the same one Hollis was staying at—Mallory and Baxter's journey to their room was made in complete silence. A silence so awkward that Mallory wanted to turn around, run for the car and speed away from Brasov—and Baxter—as fast as the motor's engine would allow.

She'd been made aware of the fact that they'd be expected to pose as a couple while in the city, where others could potentially be watching their target, too. But she hadn't expected to be booked into a *double* room. Just sharing a room was bad enough, but the same bed? Either that was all that was available, or it was someone at HQ's idea of a joke. Either way, Mallory knew she wouldn't be getting much sleep for the next couple of nights—and not for the fun reason.

Ever the gentleman, Baxter unlocked and opened the door, then held it open for her. She flashed him a grateful smile and entered the room. Almost immediately, her heart sunk. *Bloody hell—can this get any worse?* Far from the clean but purely functional accommodation she'd expected, the place was stunning. The lobby of the old building had been very nicely decorated in keeping with the age of the place, but the rooms—or this bedroom, anyway—were above and beyond that. It could only be described as sumptuous. It wasn't lavish in the same way as the room she'd last shared with Baxter, back in Amsterdam, but was beautiful nonetheless. It was old-fashioned, with lots of dark wood, flocked wallpaper, a large, wood-framed mirror, lovely artwork and pretty plants. But the *pièce de résistance*, undoubtedly, was the four-poster bed. *Fucking hell, what is this, the honeymoon suite?* It positively dripped with class and romance. In different circumstances it would be amazing, but it was *not* what she was looking for right now.

Working hard not to let her emotions show, she breezed across the room and put her bag down in front of the wardrobe. She heard the door close. When she turned around, all smiles, Baxter was crossing the room. He peered at the bed, then shifted his gaze to her. His face was definitely *not* all smiles. Pointing his chin in the direction of the—fortunately quite large—sofa, he said, "Don't worry, I'll sleep on there."

Automatically, she opened her mouth to protest, but Baxter

cut her off. "Mallory, I won't hear of it. I get that we have to share a room to maintain our cover, but no one but us is going to know if I sleep on the sofa. And it *will* be me. I'll have none of your excuses about you being smaller or whatever you were going to come up with. It's plenty big enough, and it looks quite comfortable, actually. So that's settled then."

He was being bossy again, but this time it didn't make her want to slap him. More like shag him. Senseless. Fighting hard to tamp down her burgeoning arousal, she said, "Fine." Then, remembering her manners, added, "Thank you. It's very nice of you. I appreciate it."

She paused, then launched into business mode. "So, we should get on with it, then. We already know that Hollis is staying in this hotel. According to our sources he's not in the building at the moment—but has only gone out for dinner. We don't need to worry about catching up to him just yet, I don't think. Before we latch on to him, we should make ourselves look touristy. It's imperative we blend in, in case he's watching out for someone following him, or his Russian associate has someone watching him to make sure he's not being followed. We don't want to risk spooking the guy he's meeting, or it's all over."

Baxter smirked. "That's a lot of watching and following. But I think I follow."

"Smart arse."

"Yep. So, how do we make ourselves look touristy?"

Glancing at Baxter's attire—jeans and a T-shirt—at the same time trying not to think about the delicious body that was underneath, she said, "Outfit-wise, we're golden. We'll empty out our backpacks of everything but the essentials and put them on. Then maybe one of us should go and buy a cap from a souvenir shop or something. Our phones can act as maps and tourist information, so we're all good there. First, though, I just need to freshen up. Won't be a mo."

Ten minutes later, they were out on the street. A further ten minutes later and Baxter's blond locks were covered by a navy blue baseball cap emblazoned with the word *Romania* in red script. Mallory smirked. "Looks great, Clark. And it'll keep the sun off your head, too."

Baxter frowned slightly at her first use of his cover name, but quickly recovered. Returning her smirk, he said, "Thanks, Bea. Glad you like it." He slipped his arm around her waist and pulled her close, then dropped a kiss on the top of her head. "Ready to go and get some dinner? Do you want to check that app you downloaded for local recommendations?"

Before leaving the relative safety of their hotel room, they'd decided to err on the side of caution. Hollis and his contact probably had no idea whatsoever that anyone was on to them, but just in case, Mallory and Baxter would fully embrace their loved-up-tourists cover, and use coded language wherever possible. Therefore, she knew what he really meant was *Check your phone to see if we've been sent the location of where our target is eating.*

Gently pulling away from his embrace and resolutely concentrating on anything *but* the effect his proximity had had on her, she smiled and said, "Good idea. And yes, I'm starving." She was, too—breakfast had been a long time ago and the sudden hurry to get to Romania meant she'd been forced to eat lunch on the plane—never a taste bud-pleasing experience. She pulled her phone from her pocket and checked it. As luck would have it, there was a message.

Pizza Roma is very nice. Freshly-cooked pizzas and desserts to die for.

She tapped in a response. *Thank you for the recommendation. Clark and I will check it out.* After hitting send, she pulled up a map and found the location of the restaurant. It wasn't far, but then that wasn't a surprise. As far as they knew, Hollis hadn't been to the city before, and he didn't have a vehicle, so he was hardly likely to stray too far from the hotel.

Nodding, she looked up at Baxter. "Got it. Fancy a pizza?"

"Right now, I'm so hungry I could eat anything, but pizza sounds good. Lead the way, sweetheart."

Mallory returned her phone to her pocket, then slipped her hand into Baxter's. It felt weird but good all at once, and she hoped that the longer they playacted, the more she would settle into it. She'd never had a problem before—even with a colleague she *wasn't* attracted to—but then, the current situation with her and Baxter was much more complex than merely being colleagues, wasn't it? Ultimately, though, it didn't matter what she was feeling on the inside. As long as to the outside world she looked like a woman in love, and not a spook faking it in order to blend in while following someone, all would be well.

As they walked into what looked to be the main town square, Mallory took in their surroundings. Partly because it was her job, naturally, but also because the surroundings were well worth looking at. It was a large, open space, immaculately kept, with beautiful buildings and views up into the hills on either side. The fact the whole scene was bathed in evening sunshine likely highlighted its aesthetically pleasing qualities, but Mallory still found herself wishing she *was* just a simple tourist, here to explore. Brasov looked to be an excellent place for a holiday, and she'd barely seen any of it yet.

Despite her slight distraction, her instincts were still bang on, and she hadn't so far noticed anyone or anything to worry her. But she remained vigilant as they crossed the pretty square and headed down the biggest street leading off of it, in the direction of the pizza place. As her stomach rumbled, she mentally kept her fingers crossed that their target would hang around long enough that they'd actually be able to eat something. If they had to wait until he'd gone to bed, their food choices would be severely limited.

A few minutes later, she and Baxter were being shown up a flight of stairs with a wrought-iron balustrade into the seating area of the restaurant, which was a mezzanine with a view down to the kitchen below and out onto the street. Any normal person would be eager to sit at the balcony end and enjoy the view. However, that's where their target was seated, and although it would be impossible for him not to notice them at all, they didn't want to get *too* familiar.

"Oh!" Mallory jumped in and gently touched the waitress' arm as she started to lead them in that direction. "Would it be okay to sit back here somewhere, please?"

A look of confusion flitted across the young woman's face, but was hurriedly replaced with a smile. "Of course—wherever you like." She took a couple of steps over to a table at the back and indicated it. "This is okay for you? You do not like heights?"

"This is great, thank you," Mallory said, taking the seat that Baxter had pulled out for her, before rounding the table and taking his own seat. "I…" She glanced over at Baxter, then back to the waitress. "*We,* wanted to sit somewhere *quieter.*" She beamed widely at the woman, then reached out and took Baxter's hands where they rested on the table, hoping she reached the conclusion Mallory had been aiming for—that the two of them couldn't keep their hands off each other and therefore preferred to sit somewhere more private.

"Here are your menus." The waitress returned her smile and handed the two of them their menus. "What can I get you to drink?"

Without looking at the menu, Mallory said, "A Diet Coke, please."

"It is Pepsi—that is okay?"

"That's fine."

"Large or small?"

She'd better stick with a small one, just in case they did need to make a hasty exit from the restaurant. The last thing she wanted was an overly full bladder when the chance to relieve herself might not present itself for some time. "Small, please."

The woman inclined her head, then turned to Baxter. "And for you, sir?"

"The same, please."

"Very good. I will be right back with your drinks."

Mallory smiled her thanks, then turned her attention to Baxter, but also taking thorough stock of Hollis in her peripheral vision. "So, let's have a look at this menu. I'm sure she'll be back soon with our drinks and I'd prefer to order then, since my stomach's started rumbling like crazy!"

It was true, but at the same time she was covertly telling Baxter she didn't want to hang around too long, just in case their target made a move.

From the look on his face, he understood her perfectly. Giving her an indulgent smile, he replied, "Okay, I'll hurry. I'm starving, too." He paused. "Whatever they're cooking right now smells *delicious*."

Breathing in through her nostrils, Mallory had to agree. "Yes, it does." She closed her eyes for a moment as the delicious scents seeped through her system and made her mouth water. Then, as the ramifications hit her brain, her heart leapt. Given Hollis was the only other customer—it was maybe a little bit late to be having dinner—it had to be his food they were currently preparing, so perhaps they weren't as far behind him as they thought. Or maybe he'd had a starter, or taken a long time to decide. Either way, they had more time than they thought to scope him out. *Excellent.*

Deciding on a *quattro formaggi*, Mallory closed her menu and, with a surreptitious glance over at Hollis, slipped her phone from her pocket. She had to be absolutely sure it was him before they went any further. A quick visual check confirmed it, so she pulled up a new message to HQ, then typed,

Found the restaurant. Smells great in here! Thanks for the tip—I'm sure we're going to enjoy it. Looking forward to an explore of the city once we're done eating.

Okay, now HQ knew they'd located their target, had eyes on and were ready to follow. Any further contact wouldn't be necessary unless they had anything to report, or if any vital information came to light, or they needed any kind of support or backup.

For now, all they had to do was eat and drink, remain vigilant, and be ready to react when Hollis left the restaurant.

Chapter Eighteen

"Well," Baxter said as he closed the hotel room door behind them, "I'm really glad we got to finish that delicious meal, because otherwise I'd say the day has been a bit of a waste of time. The bloke had a meal and has now gone to bed—not even a sniff of illegal activity."

Mallory shot him an amused glance as she took off her backpack and put it down on the sofa. Then, remembering that was Baxter's bed for the night, she moved it onto the floor. "It's not all guns, jet-setting, secret lairs and hot chicks, you know. We're not in a James Bond film."

He crossed the room, shucking his own backpack, and placed it beside hers. "Oh, I dunno," he said with a shrug, "I've had a hot chick on my arm all day, and now I've got her all alone in a lovely hotel room with a four-poster bed. Could be worse."

Mallory rolled her eyes even as her heart skipped a beat. God, was he really going there, or was he just being his usual flirtatious self? Walking over to the drawer where she'd stashed her clean clothes, she decided that the best response was none at all. She'd get into less trouble that way. Maybe.

She retrieved her nightwear, thankful that she wasn't the type to wear skimpy pyjamas. If she was *planning* on having an overnight guest, well, that was different—and lingerie, rather than pyjamas, was generally the order of the day. Or should that be night? But for the go-bags she kept ready for days such as this one, it was sleepwear all the way. Emphasis on sleep.

What Baxter chose to wear for bed was another matter entirely. Just because she'd be fairly demurely dressed—it was a cute T-shirt and short trousers set, not a Victorian neck-to-ankle nightgown—didn't mean that he wouldn't be temptation personified. She was mostly certain that he wouldn't sleep naked, but although swanning around in a pair of boxer shorts was hardly obscene, she and her tortured hormones hoped that he would at least wear a T-shirt, too. Perhaps she could insist, telling him it was a matter of national security. It was, really. After all, if the sight of him with no shirt on frustrated her to the point that her head exploded, then that would put their entire operation at risk, and consequently, national security. She'd have trouble doing her job if she was dead.

That decided, she turned and headed towards the bathroom.

She'd just put her hand on the door handle when Baxter said, "I dunno why you're bothering going in there. It's not like I haven't seen it all before."

Once again, she didn't respond—instead darting inside the bathroom and closing and locking the door behind her. She placed her pyjamas down beside the sink, then rested her hands on the cool marble surface and peered at herself in the mirror. She looked… perfectly fine, actually. What had she been expecting? Her face to somehow be displaying the confusion and turmoil going on inside? She'd spent years training and practising so that very thing *wouldn't* happen. She'd remained outwardly calm and collected whilst rubbing shoulders with some of the scariest people on the planet— why the hell would Baxter Collinson be the one to ruffle her feathers? Granted, the former were dangerous people. The only danger that Baxter posed was to her heart.

Letting out an exasperated snort, she took off her clothes and put on the pyjamas. Then she used the toilet and washed her hands and face, before brushing her teeth. After putting her toiletries back into her wash bag, she knew she couldn't delay any longer, so she collected the pile of discarded clothes and went back into the bedroom.

Baxter—much to her relief—was fully clothed. His nightwear, apparently, consisted of T-shirt and shorts. He'd gotten himself settled onto the sofa with his tablet; a blanket he'd found bundled up by his feet. Two bottles of water sat on the table beside him.

She hung up the clothes she'd need for tomorrow, then stashed the stuff that needed laundering away. Taking a deep breath, she approached the table. "Is one of those for me?"

Baxter looked up, then followed her gaze to the bottles. "Yes, of course. There were more exciting things in the mini-bar, but I'm not sure what the stance is on drinking on the job. *Are* we currently on the job? Or are we off-duty? I'm still getting the hang of all this."

She grabbed a bottle and flashed him a grateful smile before dropping into the armchair which sat at ninety degrees from the sofa. "Thank you. And you will get the hang of it, I promise. To answer your question, probably the best way to describe what we are right now is on call. We're not working at this very second in time, but we have to be ready to mobilise at a moment's notice. I think we're safe for tonight, but we can't be too careful. So water is a good call." She twisted off the lid and took several long gulps before resealing it and putting it back on the table. The last time they'd been in a hotel room together, they'd been quaffing expensive champagne. But she *had* been trying to seduce him. This time, she worried that any alcohol in her system—however small an amount—might lower her inhibitions and allow her to give in to the chemistry that constantly simmered between them, despite all her efforts to ignore it.

Baxter nodded. "Great. So, uh, are you tired yet? Despite the travelling, I'm not ready to sleep yet—my body clock is still firmly two hours behind. I reckon if we got tucked up and turned off the lights, I'd end up staring at the insides of my eyelids."

"Not really." She shook her head, trying not to think about *them*—as in him and her—being tucked up. She knew that hadn't been what he meant, but her brain still wanted to go there, apparently. "But it's not like we can go sightseeing at this time of night, is it?"

"No—though I'm sure Bran Castle would be creepy as anything in the dark!"

"I'm sure." She gave a small smile. "So, unless you've bought a travel-sized game of Monopoly or Scrabble with you, I think I'm going to grab my Kindle and read for a bit."

"Or…" he replied, halting her as she was halfway to standing. "We could just… talk."

She plopped back into the chair, her heart suddenly pounding and a sick feeling taking over her stomach. "A-about what?"

He gave her a narrow-eyed look. "You know what, Mallory. Come on, you have to stop avoiding this—it's not doing either of us any favours. Why is it that a woman who wades into insanely dangerous situations on a regular basis for her job is frightened of having a conversation about, well, whatever it is that we are?"

"We're colleagues," she shot back.

He glared. "*All right,* a conversation about what happened between us before, then. Seriously, I think you owe me this, at least. Was anything about it fucking real, or not?"

Mallory dropped her head into her hands. Then, after a moment, she looked up at him. "Do you really think now is a good time to talk about this? I know we're on call, as I put it, but if this turns into a row, people might hear, and we're supposed to be a loved-up couple, remember? If we're not even on speaking terms tomorrow, nobody is going to believe that cover story."

Baxter rolled his eyes. "Bullshit. I'm sure we can have a conversation without it turning into a slanging match. Plus, nobody will give a flying fuck if we're not on speaking terms tomorrow—it might even be more realistic. All couples argue—especially on holiday when they're spending twenty-four hours a day together, unlike at home when they have jobs and things to go to."

"Oh, I'm sorry," she replied, her voice dripping with sarcasm, "I didn't realise you were such an expert on relationships. If that's the case, why bother talking at all? You obviously already know exactly what's been going on."

He leaned forward and placed his tablet on the table, then ran his hands through his hair and let out a low growl. "Fucking hell, Mallory, you can be seriously infuriating at times. Fine—if you want to be like that, here's what I think. I think that, back in Amsterdam, it started out as a job for you, obviously. But then when we spent a little time together, you enjoyed yourself, enjoyed my company. And at some point, the line between screwing me for intelligence purposes and screwing me because you wanted to became incredibly blurred. Almost unrecognisable, in fact."

He paused for a moment and took a shaky breath, then continued, "You started to feel guilty about what you were doing, but figured it didn't matter—once you'd got what you wanted, you'd have your guys swoop in and take me and the others down, then you'd never have to see me again. And then it all went tits up when I ended up being offered a job in your section. That was bad enough, but then you were put in charge of me. So you had to see me all the time. Train me, test me, whatever. And any… feelings you had for me, instead of being allowed to fade away as I rotted in prison, were placed front and centre, leaving you unable to escape. Hence you keeping me at arm's length ever since the moment I walked out of your hotel room. I'm guessing that any… relationships between colleagues are against the rules."

Fucking hell, is he a mind reader or something? Her horror had stunned her into silence, leaving her unable to do anything but gape at him.

"What's the matter—cat got your tongue? Or did I just hit the nail on the head?"

The urge to slap him now was so strong that her right palm tingled. Perhaps it was as well she wasn't armed. "Fuck, Baxter, did you swallow a book of clichés, or what?"

He smirked. "Really? That's the best response you could come up with?"

She knew he was deliberately trying to goad her, but she didn't want to give him the satisfaction of agreeing with him. Though he clearly already knew he was right—otherwise why would he have said all that? The trouble was, his being right didn't mean anything. Not a bloody thing. Yes, he had indeed hit the nail on the head, but it didn't change the fact that nothing could ever happen between them. Baxter Collinson was firmly out of bounds. Forbidden fruit. And… God, now who'd swallowed a book of clichés?

Mallory sighed. "Baxter, what do you want me to say? Just tell me and we'll get it over and done with."

"I just want the truth, Mallory. Was everything I just said right? Or even some of it? *Do* you have feelings for me, or was I literally just part of the job? Because, just to lay my cards on the table—maybe you're right about swallowing that book—I meant what I said back in that interrogation room. You could have had me—you *can* have me. I'm crazy about you, Mallory Scott, and not even you targeting me and my gang, then getting me arrested and almost thrown in jail has changed that. I'm not entirely sure what that means, but it's got to be important. And powerful. And… for fuck's sake, would you just say something?"

"Oh!" she replied, jumping up. "Was that my phone?"

Chapter Nineteen

Mallory had barely taken two steps before Baxter caught up to her. He grabbed her wrist firmly—but not enough to hurt—and spun her around to face him. His eyebrows were drawn down low, and his eyes glinted with anger. "Mallory," he said quietly, his dark tone sending a chill running down her spine, "please would you stop avoiding this? Christ, do you want me to beg? And don't give me that shit about your phone—I know as well as you do that it didn't make a bloody sound. Thing's loud enough to wake the dead."

"Please would you let go of me?" she said breathlessly. She wasn't sure exactly *why* she was breathless. Was it his proximity, the fact he'd caught her out in a lie, or that he was demanding she talk about something she *really* didn't want to?

He released her wrist, but still held her firmly in his darkened gaze. "All I'm asking for is the truth, Mallory. I just want to *know*. Maybe then I can start to get my head straight."

The anger in his eyes had morphed into a mixture of sadness and pain, and it made her heart sink and thump hard at the same time. The worst part was knowing he was right—she did owe him this. Yes, he'd done wrong in the past, but he was trying to make up for it now. Also, regardless of his past, he was a human being with thoughts, feelings and emotions, and she was toying—albeit without malice—with them. Because she was scared.

Suddenly, she wasn't sure she was the most moral person in the room—and when the other one used to steal and forge diamonds for a living, that was definitely not a good thing. Straightening her spine and drawing in a deep breath, she reached out and took his hand. "I…" She huffed loudly. "Baxter, I… I'm sorry. You *do* deserve the truth. I'm being a coward. It's no excuse, but I'm not used to this kind of thing. I'm used to dealing with bad people and being brave in the face of danger, but this," she waved her free hand between the two of them, "is way out of my comfort zone. Christ—I wish I could have a drink! I could do with one right about now."

Baxter chuckled, his expression lightening. "Dutch courage?"

"Yes, Mr Cliché. Dutch courage. I bloody well need it."

With a squeeze of her hand, Baxter tugged her gently back towards the sofa. "Come on, let's sit down."

She followed, then sat down beside him, their hands still linked. She sighed. "I'm overcomplicating this massively in my head, you know. Which is ridiculous, when you consider how easy you made it." Pausing, she reached for his other hand. Their gazes met and held. "Yes, Baxter. You hit the nail directly on the head. Everything you said is accurate—which is why I've been keeping you at arm's length. Because I want to… and we can't…"

"Because of the job?" he asked quietly.

"Y-yes." She sniffed. "It's all completely fucked up, if you ask me. We're posing as a couple, sharing a fucking bedroom, for Christ's sake, but if we were to become a *real* couple, we'd be hauled across the coals back at the office. Or I would be, anyway. They might just renege on your offer and throw you in prison. So you see, it doesn't really matter what *we* want, because it can't happen."

Baxter raised his eyebrows. "It can't?"

Frowning, Mallory replied, "Of course it can't. Didn't you hear what I just said? Do you *want* to go to prison?"

"I heard every word. But what if nobody *knew* we were a couple?"

"What?" she squeaked, then immediately spluttered out a laugh. "Are you proposing we sneak around behind their backs? I'm not sure if you've noticed, but we're in the espionage business."

"Which, surely, gives us—or you, at any rate—the best possible skill set needed to *sneak around behind their backs,* as you so delicately put it."

"If I was cheating on an unsuspecting husband or something, then yeah, we'd be able to pull it off. But we're trying to hide something from the very people that employ me—and soon, you—to spy, and lie, and pretend to be other people. They'd work it out before we'd even kissed."

"We've already kissed. And a whole lot more besides." He gave a lopsided smile, and the glint in his eye was now most definitely in mischievous territory.

She groaned and shoved his hands away, even as sexy memories started to tickle at the edges of her consciousness. "You know what I mean. I just don't see, even with the best will in the world, how we could possibly keep it from them."

"We'd be careful—even more careful than careful—and smart. And—"

"Baxter."

"What?"

"Don't." She dropped her head into her hands again for a moment, then lifted it and looked up at him. "Please don't make this more difficult than it already is. For both of our sakes. I think we should move on from this and try and forget about it. It just can't happen, no matter how much we want it to. I'm sorry."

"Yeah," he replied, slumping heavily back into the sofa, "me too. This fucking sucks." He crossed his arms and pouted. Mallory was just on the verge of telling him he looked like a sulky child when his expression transformed entirely—to a huge, beaming grin and eyes wide with wonder. *Oh, Christ, he's thought of something.* She could practically see the light bulb above his head. This was going to be trouble—she could feel it.

In spite of her trepidation, she tried—and failed—to stifle her own smile. "What? What the hell did you just think of? You've gone from looking like a kid who just had his toys taken away, to a kid on Christmas morning."

He turned to face her again, still beaming. "Let's not talk about kids right now, okay? What I have in mind is most definitely *not* family friendly."

She rolled her eyes and said in a resigned tone, "Go on…"

"It's a little out of the ordinary, but then, you are no ordinary woman. And I figure at this stage I've got nothing to lose—"

"Baxter! Will you just get on with it?"

"All right, all right! Just…" he paused. "You definitely aren't armed, are you?" He eyed her worriedly.

"No, definitely not. And if I was, where the hell would I stash a weapon in this outfit?"

"Good point."

"Just because I haven't got a gun, doesn't mean I can't kill you, though."

"I realise that, but I might at least have a fighting chance if you're not carrying a weapon. *Anyway…* here's my idea. Please resist the temptation to kill me—that would *definitely* blow our cover. How about a last hurrah?"

"A last… hurrah?" She frowned. "I don't follow." He wanted a celebration?

"I can see that. I've never seen you look so confused. What I'm suggesting is… why don't we move on from this by having a last hurrah, then drawing a line under it? And by last hurrah, I mean—"

Suddenly, the penny dropped. "Yes, Baxter, I think I've got it now. You're saying, to be blunt, that we should have one last sex session to… what… get it out of our systems, then never speak of it again."

"Correct. Except by session, I mean the whole night. Not just the once. Why sell ourselves short?" He waggled his eyebrows. "You know we can do better than that."

Snorting, she shook her head. "You're bloody mad, you know that?"

Baxter's expression turned innocent. "What? What's mad about that? Sex is *always* a good idea."

"Not when the background and circumstances are as complicated as ours. Much as I'm a fan of a good shag, I think we'd be playing with fire."

"A *good* shag?" he said indignantly. "I think what you mean is a *spectacular* shag, right?"

"You really need me to massage your ego?"

His eyebrows drew together. "Humph. I suppose not. And as for the playing with fire—how so? Nobody but us will ever know what happened. We're mature adults, we can handle it."

The more they talked about it, the more the memories she'd been trying to keep at bay flitted through her mind, getting increasingly hotter. *Fuck's sake—why does he have to be so bloody tempting?* "Fine."

"F-fine?" His eyebrows shot up in surprise. "Is that a yes-let's-do-it fine?"

"Yes." Doubt still coursed through her, particularly as when she'd mentioned playing with fire, she hadn't meant with work. She'd meant with their emotions, their hearts. But hey—hers were already in a mess, so they could hardly get much worse, right?

"Wow." Baxter blew out a heavy breath and ran a hand through his hair. "I didn't think that persuasion would actually work. Maybe I should become a lawyer."

"Surely this isn't the first time you've talked a woman into sleeping with you?"

"It is, actually. And I couldn't be happier that my first time was with you."

Mallory shook her head. "Any more of that and I might just change my mind. You know how I feel about your cheesy chat-up lines."

"In that case, I'll shut up. If I don't say anything, I can't get it wrong."

"You mean you're going to keep quiet from now until we've done the deed? You'll never last that long!" She remembered the last time they'd been in a similar situation, when she'd begged him to stop talking and fuck her. He hadn't kept quiet, exactly, but he had *definitely* fucked her.

Baxter smirked and drew his fingertips across his lips in a zipping-it-closed action. Perhaps he, too, was remembering what had happened before. He got up from the sofa and held a hand out to her. Raising her eyebrows in amusement, Mallory took it and allowed him to lead her over to the bed. With every step, her heart beat faster and heat grew between her legs.

By the time he pushed her gently onto the mattress—which was surprisingly comfortable considering the apparent vintage of the bed itself—all the doubts and questions and what-ifs that had been whirling around her mind had disappeared. Instead, it was full of the anticipation, the need, born of the restraint she'd been showing for the last couple of weeks. She'd always been of the opinion that denying herself her favourite foods because they were bad for her was a stupid idea, because when she cracked, instead of just eating a little, she'd gorge herself silly because she'd deprived herself for so long. It seemed this situation wouldn't be any different. Baxter was bad for her—in more ways than one—but her craving for him had never gone away. If anything, it had intensified. Now she had this one opportunity to gorge herself on him, and she was going to take it.

The question was, would they both emerge unscathed?

There was only one way to find out.

Chapter Twenty

Baxter quickly followed Mallory onto the bed, straddling her and placing his hands on either side of her head. He paused for a few seconds, looking down at her with a wide smile before leaning in for a kiss.

She let out a loud moan as their lips touched, and she felt Baxter's mouth twist into a smile. It was just as well he'd sworn himself to silence, because he no doubt had a smart arse comment hovering on the tip of his tongue. Well, she'd make sure to keep his tongue busy for as long as humanly possible, so by the time he was allowed to speak, he'd hopefully have forgotten about her apparent eagerness.

Reaching up with both hands, she tangled them in his hair and pulled him harder onto her, deepening their kiss. Lust zinged wildly through her body, centring not only in the obvious erogenous zones, but making her tingle all over. Being with him was familiar yet exciting, and she could hardly wait to rediscover what he looked and felt like beneath the T-shirt and shorts.

They continued to explore each other's mouths at a steady yet thorough pace, as though the knowledge that this was a one-time-only deal was forcing them to savour the experience. Shifting one of her hands down his back, she then slipped it beneath his T-shirt and enjoyed the sensation of his firm muscles. She lightly scraped her fingernails across his warm skin, causing him to break away from their kiss with a gasp. He opened his mouth to say something, but she quickly put a finger to his lips, reminding him of their agreement.

Nodding and smiling, Baxter dipped his head again, but this time focussed his attention on her neck, her jaw line, her ears. He nibbled at the delicate lobes, then tongued them lightly, making her writhe on the mattress as arousal pumped through her, increasing in intensity with every second that passed. Already she was eager for them to be naked, skin to skin, and for them to be joined, rocking and thrusting their way to their respective climaxes.

She moved her hands down to squeeze his buttocks through his shorts. He nipped at her earlobe in response, making her gasp, then immediately slipped his hands beneath the hem of her T-shirt and pushed it up beneath her breasts. He soon homed in on the exposed skin, pressing kisses to it and running his tongue over her stomach, gradually working his way higher, until he was forced to shove the cotton material right up to her neck.

"Wait!" she said, with a face full of T-shirt, "Let me take the bloody thing off."

Rolling off her with a grin, Baxter seemed about to say something, apparently forgetting yet again he was meant to be being quiet. She couldn't blame him, really. The lust building inside her was making it difficult for her to concentrate on anything but what they were doing, too. He kept quiet, though, and she returned his grin before whipping off her top and throwing it to one side, where it glanced off one of the bedposts and tumbled to the carpet.

To her surprise, Baxter didn't advance on her. Instead, he got off the bed and made short work of removing his own clothes. It didn't take long, so she was soon treated to the delectable view of a naked, gorgeous Baxter. Hardly realising she was doing it, she licked her lips as she raked her gaze up and down his body, before allowing it to linger on his cock. Oh yeah, he was just as sexy as she remembered.

She finally managed to tear her focus from his dick and shifted it up to his face, which still wore a grin—which had now turned wicked. Raising his eyebrows, he pointed his chin towards her cropped trousers and gave her a meaningful look—his silent way of telling her to take them off.

Mallory complied, hooking her thumbs into the waistband of the trousers and tugging them down, shimmying and then lifting her hips at the relevant moment. Once they were around her ankles, she pulled one foot free and used the other to flick the garment off and in Baxter's direction. Her aim was terrible, almost nonexistent, and they flew past his head and landed on the dresser. He glanced around to see where they'd landed, then turned back to her, shaking his head and smirking.

She stuck out her tongue, then quickly pulled it back in as a thought occurred to her. "Hey, while you're up," she couldn't resist another peek at his erection as the unintended double entendre popped out, "go grab some condoms, would you? Do you have any?"

Giving her a look that indicated she'd just asked the stupidest question known to man, Baxter turned on his heel and walked across to where he'd left his backpack. Glad she didn't have to get up from her comfortable position on the bed to retrieve her own stash of protection, she remained precisely where she was, enjoying the view as he sauntered away. Strong biceps, wide shoulders and back, tapering down into well proportioned hips. And those long, lean, muscular legs, capped by the pert globes of his perfect backside—*yum*. She was definitely going to make the most of him and his hot body tonight, while she had the chance. Then it would be back into professional mode and full steam ahead on the mission tomorrow.

Ugh. She didn't want to think about work right now, important as it was. Thankfully, when Baxter turned and headed back towards the bed, his right hand curled around what she assumed was the condoms, all thoughts of, well, anything but those condoms and what they were going to be used for flew out of her head. She looked him up and down again, committing the impossibly erotic images to memory.

Baxter placed the handful of foil packets on the nearest bedside table, then the mattress dipped as he climbed up beside her once more. As soon as he was close enough, she hooked an arm around his neck and drew him in for a kiss. Last time they'd been together it had been impulsive, fast, and furious, with their only foreplay being the intense flirting they'd done up until the point when they decided to sleep together. Mallory was determined it would be different this time around. They had privacy, and they had all night, so could indulge in as much foreplay as they wanted, and as many positions as their fertile imaginations provided.

For now, though, she had something very simple and straightforward in mind. She enjoyed the kiss for a while longer, then pulled back. With a grin, she said, "Lie back," and gave his shoulder a little push.

Baxter bit his lip—she wasn't sure whether it was because he'd worked out what she had in mind, or with the effort of keeping quiet—and did as she'd commanded, settling in amongst the plentiful pillows. She scooted into position between his legs, smirking at the sight of his cock standing proudly to attention. Turned out Baxter didn't need to say a word to make it clear how aroused he was.

Reaching out and closing her hand around his eager erection, she hummed with pleasure at the heat and hardness beneath her fingers. She shunted her hand up and down his shaft a few times, loving how it felt, how it lengthened and thickened as a result of her ministrations, and even more how it made Baxter groan and jerk his hips, encouraging her. She licked her lips, then again, making sure they were good and wet before leaning down and closing them around the head of Baxter's cock. He moaned again and she quickly pressed her forearms onto his inner thighs to keep him still. She didn't want him bucking up into her mouth—she wanted to be in control, especially as she took him deeper. Everything was so up close and personal by now that she shut her eyes.

Sucking lightly on just the tip of Baxter's cock, Mallory enjoyed his flavour as it seeped from him and coated her taste buds. She teased him by concentrating on the sensitive area beneath the crown, using her lips and tongue to stimulate it, and deliberately allowing her saliva to dribble down his length. She'd need it soon enough. Her mouth wasn't the only thing producing wetness, either. Even though her full concentration—for now—was on sucking Baxter's cock, she was still incredibly turned on. In fact, the act of giving him head was actually making her hornier.

Pausing momentarily to draw in a deep, steadying breath through her nostrils, she then upped her game, and the pace. Chasing the natural lubricant down Baxter's cock, she carefully licked and sucked until it was coated, then began bobbing her head up and down. The saliva meant she glided smoothly and easily, and she hollowed out her cheeks, increasing the suction, gratified when the action drew out yet more sounds of pleasure from her lover.

She smiled to herself and moved faster, simulating the movements they'd be making if they were fucking. Up and down, up and down. Hot. Hard. Slick. So. Fucking. Sexy.

The taste of precum hit her once more, and she shifted a hand down to cup and lightly tug at his balls, silently letting him know that it was perfectly okay with her if he came in her mouth. Right at that very moment, she couldn't think of anything she wanted more. Except maybe an orgasm of her own—but she was confident that would follow soon after his. He wouldn't leave her hanging. He wouldn't dare.

Baxter's sounds and movements grew more frantic, even frenzied. It was clear he was on the very edge of climax. She slipped her index finger beneath his ball sac and stroked the smooth patch of skin there, stopping just short of his arsehole.

That was all it took: Baxter let go. She continued what she was doing, but opened her eyes and looked up the bed so she could see him as he came. His hands gripped the duvet and his torso was tense. But it was the expression on his face that was almost her undoing—it was full of intense concentration, his mouth squeezed tightly closed.

Then everything happened at once. His balls drew up towards his body and his shaft grew harder still—which she hadn't even thought was possible. Then, just as he started to twitch and deposit his load in her mouth, he groaned deeply and loudly and his face took on an expression of pure serenity. He looked almost angelic. It was the sensation of release, she supposed. Baxter Collinson was far from angelic.

She kept her lips fastened securely around his cock as the salty cum spurted out, swallowing rapidly to keep her mouth from overflowing.

When it had finally stopped, she pulled away with a grin and wiped her mouth on the back of her hand. Then, determined to keep him quiet for a little longer, she crawled up the bed, looking for all the world as though she was going to cuddle up next to him. Instead, she gripped the sturdy headboard and swung one leg over his head, straddling his face.

Much to Baxter's credit, after a single grunt of confusion as his post-climax brain apparently caught up with events, he reached up and cupped her arse cheeks before burying his tongue into her slick pout.

Chapter Twenty-One

Mallory was immediately glad that the headboard *was* sturdy, because Baxter had a *very* talented tongue, and he sure knew how to use it. Therefore she needed something to keep her upright, otherwise she'd fall over or end up squashing Baxter's face. And it was *way* too pretty a face to risk that.

His enthusiasm indicated that he genuinely enjoyed going down on a woman, rather than just doing it out of politeness, habit or pressure. He danced his tongue in her swollen folds, licking up her juices as he teased and titillated her. After a while, he shifted his attention to her clit, gently sucking on it at first, then gradually upping the pressure as the tiny bud grew and throbbed.

Breathing heavily, she let her head loll back and her eyes flutter closed as pleasure began to build in her abdomen. Baxter had released her clit, and was now using his tongue to alternately circle it and flick back and forth, then side to side. Juices continued to trickle from her pussy, no doubt coating his lips and chin.

Mallory tightened her grip on the headboard as she hovered on the very edge of climax. Then she sunk her teeth into her bottom lip as Baxter closed his mouth around her nub once more. As soon as he started to suck it, her orgasm hit. She bit down harder to avoid making a noise—she didn't want the guests in the neighbouring rooms to hear her cries. Even now, in the midst of overwhelming bliss, she was aware of drawing unwanted attention. Soon she could remain silent no more, but managed to keep the strangled moans, gasps and expletives to a relatively low volume as sparks ran through her entire body and her internal walls clenched around nothing. But hopefully not for long.

Finally, as the waves of ecstasy subsided, she managed to clamber off Baxter without accidentally kicking or kneeing him in the head, and collapsed to the mattress beside him with a wide grin.

Baxter turned his head to look at her, his expression mirroring her own. Except his wide grin, and all the skin surrounding it, was smeared with her juices. He licked his lips, then reached out and cupped her cheek before pulling her in for a kiss. She went willingly, and the taste of herself on him fired up her lust all over again.

She slid her hand down his body and sought his cock, pleased to find it red hot and rock hard—most definitely ready to go again.

She stroked it gently as they continued kissing, wanting to pleasure him without making him come—the next time he did that she wanted him to be inside her. *Deep* inside.

Before long their kisses and caresses grew frantic, and Mallory pulled away gasping for air, her brain fuzzy with lust. She continued lightly pumping her hand up and down Baxter's shaft. Smiling at him, she said, "I think you'd better grab one of those condoms, before it's too late."

With a nod and a smirk, he rolled away from her and retrieved a packet from the pile he'd placed on the bedside table. He quickly opened it, tossed the wrapper to the floor and donned the latex. After ensuring the protection was fitted correctly, Baxter relaxed back on the bed and turned his attention to Mallory, raising a querying eyebrow before nodding towards his eager cock.

Oh, so he wants me to go on top, does he? That was just fine by her—the last time they'd been together, Baxter had been on top, so she relished the opportunity to control the speed and the depth of penetration. Not to mention being able to tease him.

She moved swiftly into position, perching for a moment on his lower abdomen—smearing his skin with yet more of her juices—before rising to her knees and reaching for his cock. Holding it firmly in position, she manoeuvred so the head was slotted between her labia, but not penetrating her. She paused there, then raked her gaze up his prone, luscious body, admiring his smooth skin and hard muscles, before finally making eye contact.

With a smile, she asked, "You ready?"

Baxter nodded emphatically and reached up to palm her breasts, but she smacked his hands away. "Ah-ah, not right now, mister. You wanted me to go on top, so I'm calling the shots."

With a huff, he dropped his hands to the bed sheets. Then, seemingly not knowing what to do with them, folded them behind his head.

His moody expression amused Mallory so much that she decided to wind him up even more—while having a great deal of fun at the same time. She slowly, so slowly she herself could barely tell she was moving, lowered herself onto Baxter's dick until just the very tip was lodged inside her, keeping her eyes on his face the entire time. He managed—but only just—to keep quiet; but his eyes widened, then closed, and he bit his lip as she tormented him with her wet warmth.

"Baxter; look at me," she commanded.

When he did, she reached up and palmed her own tits—doing the very thing she'd denied him. He watched in silence for several seconds, his eyes darkening with lust, and she sensed his internal struggle as she played with her breasts and nipples while holding his cock in limbo, neither fucking him, nor *not* fucking him. What she'd never admit, though, was that it was torturing her as much as it was him—she wanted to be fully impaled on him, have him balls-deep inside her, filling her, stretching her... fucking her to another blazing orgasm.

The thought had barely finished forming when it happened. Lightning-quick, Baxter's hands reappeared from behind his head, and he gripped her hips and pulled her down, thrusting his own hips up at the same time. His shaft slipped deeper inside her easily, given she was so wet, but she still gasped at the sudden invasion and pressure against her internal walls—as well as with the shock of it happening.

"You bastard!" she hissed, releasing her breasts and putting her hands on top of his. She dug her fingernails into his hands. "I wasn't ready."

Admirably, Baxter still didn't reply. Instead he gave a lazy shrug, then began pumping into her. Mallory failed miserably to resist, to even look as though she was unimpressed. It just felt too damn good. He might have ruined her teasing, but she was sure as hell going to wrestle back control. Grabbing his wrists, she wrenched his hands off her hips and then leaned forward and pinned his arms against the pillows on either side of his head.

Baxter didn't fight back, but he *did* stop moving. She wasn't sure what would have happened if he had resisted—he was bigger than her, but she was much stronger than she looked, as well as highly trained and skilled in hand-to-hand combat. If she had to defend herself, she was very well prepared, but she'd never tested out her abilities in the bedroom. So perhaps it could have gone either way.

However, Baxter seemed to have decided to just lie there and let her do what she wanted. Mallory couldn't decide whether to be amused or pissed off by this, so she simply decided not to bother thinking about it anymore. To stop thinking altogether, in fact. She was going to make like Nike and *just do it.*

Her new position meant that her upper body was sprawled

out on top of his, his heated, hard flesh pressed against her softer form. Smiling, she tilted her head and captured Baxter's lips in a smouldering kiss. At the same time, she began slowly rolling her hips, getting into a gentle rhythm with his shaft slipping in and out of her, seeming to spark off every nerve ending along the way. She grinned to herself. What was that phrase—slow and steady wins the race? Whether she was winning or not, she had no idea, but her body certainly felt like it was. With each movement, her pubic bone ground against Baxter's, stimulating her clit as well as her pussy. As a rule, she was usually into a faster, more frantic style of fucking, but this was seriously doing it for her, too.

Maybe it was the partner that made the difference, rather than the position, style or speed?

Refusing to linger on that sentiment for even a second, Mallory decided to drive it firmly out of her head by picking up the pace. She stayed lying down on top of Baxter for now, but jerked against him faster and faster, the slickness of her pussy hugely apparent in the rude, wet sounds it made as Baxter's cock forged in and out. Adding to the delicious sensations was the scrape of her stiff nipples against Baxter's chest.

She was approaching orgasm again, and all she wanted was to go even faster, eager for a powerful climax, and to pull Baxter over the edge along with her. That meant she had to break their kiss. She also released Baxter's wrists and pressed her palms against the bed, pushing herself up and beginning to ride him furiously. Heat scorched through her, like lightning bolts reverberating endlessly beneath her skin. She tossed her head back and let out a guttural moan, which mingled in the air with the sounds that Baxter could apparently no longer hold back—he wasn't speaking, but he couldn't stay completely quiet any longer, either.

Riding him harder still, she grunted and clenched her teeth, her blood thundering through her veins and pounding in her ears. She was zoning out, able to consider nothing but the sensations she was experiencing. And *fuck,* were they amazing. Tingles started to build in her stomach, increasing rapidly with every second that passed. Soon, there was no stopping the inevitable. With a cry, she started to come. As pleasure coursed through her, she rolled her head back into its normal position and looked at Baxter's face, into his eyes.

What she saw there managed to rock her to her very core.

Unless she was mistaken—or hallucinating—the gaze that was levelled at her was the one of a man very much in love. He hadn't said as much—all he'd said was that he had feelings for her—but now she could see it there, plain as day, it thrilled and terrified her in equal measure.

Because you're in love with him, too.

Fuck! She'd known sleeping with him again was a bad idea—it was heightening her emotions. She'd managed to make him understand that them being together was impossible, but he'd countered that with talking her into bed. Mallory had only agreed because she'd felt that a damn good shag—sorry, a spectacular shag—would actually be a great way to get it out of their systems and put it behind them so they could focus on the mission, and on the future.

But she hadn't been betting on Baxter's feelings being so powerful, or her own developing so intensely. She wasn't sure exactly when she'd gone from *falling* to *in*—but it didn't really matter. What mattered was how she dealt with it now. It didn't change anything, after all. Her job made regular relationships impossible—and although hers and Baxter's wouldn't be regular, it *was* forbidden.

She forced herself back into the present. Somewhere during her climax and the simultaneous realisation and soul-searching—damn, talk about multi-tasking—Baxter had come, too, so as their respective orgasms waned, she slumped onto him, breathing heavily and resting her weight on her forearms either side of his chest for a while, until she felt ready to move.

Finally, she was. "Hey," she said, her voice sounding slurred even to her own ears, "could you, uh, take care of the condom?"

"Sure," he replied, apparently now remembering he could speak, since they'd 'done the deed'. She still couldn't believe he'd managed it. Carefully, he slipped his hand between their bodies, and his fingers clamped around the base of his cock, securing the protection in place.

She clambered off him, aware of how clumsy and ungraceful she was being, but not having the energy to do anything about it. She felt wrung out, but in a pleasant way, as post-orgasmic hormones buzzed through her system.

Flopping onto her back, she watched Baxter get off the bed and head for the nearest bin—the sight of his naked arse was rapidly becoming one of her favourites. She closed her eyes, committing it to memory.

Suddenly the mattress beside her dipped, and warm arms pulled her so she was snuggled into him, her head resting in the space between his head and shoulder. "Hey," he said quietly, "you're not falling asleep on me, are you? I thought we were going for all night, not just the once."

Mallory chuckled and opened her eyes. "Isn't it supposed to be the woman complaining about the man falling asleep? Anyway, I wasn't—I was just resting my eyes."

With a snort, Baxter replied, "Mmm-hmm, if you say so. So, since we've already established I'm the king of clichés—how was it for you?"

"Massaging egos again, are we? I would have thought it was obvious how it was for me."

"Humour me." He reached down and tickled her ribs.

Squirming and shrieking, she slapped his hand away. "All right, all right! It was, to quote you, a *spectacular shag*. What about you?"

"Likewise. Actually, spectacular doesn't really cover it, but I can't think of another word at the moment. I'll get back to you on that one."

"Fine." The word hung in the air, alone, and Mallory's heart rate picked up once more. Now was the obvious time to engage in a conversation *beyond* how it was, venturing more into *what now?* Baxter was perceptive—what if he, too, had experienced that lightning bolt of realisation as they'd made eye contact? Would he be so willing to go along with the plan of getting the sexual tension out of their systems and moving on if full-on love, rather than simple lust and mutual fondness, was on the table?

Was *she?*

Don't be such an idiot, Mallory. You know this changes nothing. You can't have him and *your career, it's as simple as that.*

Baxter cleared his throat, making her jump and her heart skip a beat before racing faster. Much more of this and the organ would explode—though at least that would get her out of this impossible situation. "Mallory? Can I ask you a question?"

Nonono not now! Please! Gulping hard, she choked out, "Yes, what is it?"

He shifted on the mattress and pushed her onto her back,

rolling on top of her. Grinning wickedly, he poked his once-again stiffening cock into her belly and asked, "Wanna do it again?"

Chapter Twenty-Two

After the sex marathon of the previous evening—which had consisted of multiple *spectacular shags,* lots of other sexy stuff and fortunately no serious or meaningful conversation—Mallory expected to wake up feeling like she'd been steam-rollered, or exhausted at the very least. But, much to her surprise, the reality was quite the opposite. She was buzzed, energised, ready to get out there and nail their target. Maybe the endorphins that had flooded her system as a result of several orgasms still lingered. Whatever it was, she wasn't about to complain—the more energetic and alert she was, the better.

She turned to nudge Baxter awake, and got a further surprise when she discovered he wasn't there. Frowning, she reached out and touched the sheets—there was residual warmth, but not much. As her senses continued to awaken, she picked up the sound of running water—apparently he was already in the shower.

Impressed, she jumped out of bed, grabbed her robe and threw it on, then went to retrieve her phone to see if any information or orders had come in while she'd been asleep. She doubted it—she always had half an ear cocked for the sound of her phone, and HQ held back from calling or sending messages during the hours they expected their agents to be asleep, unless it was urgent. Even the best agents need sleep to remain on top of their game, after all. And the only time they were permitted to put their phones on silent was when it was operationally necessary.

She didn't know what the time was, but knew it wasn't late—she never slept in, not even after the roughest of nights. And, she thought with a grin, last night had been far from rough—not in the bad sense, anyway.

Picking up the handset, she pressed the button to light up the screen. As she'd suspected, nothing had come through, but she did now know that it was just after 7 a.m. local time. Hopefully Hollis wasn't up and out yet. Unlikely, given their body clocks would still be two hours behind, on UK time, so he'd have to be an obscenely early riser. Plus, an arrangement had been put into place to alert her if he left his room before she and Baxter left theirs—and she'd heard nothing, so for now it was all good. Ideally, they'd be tucking into breakfast in the dining room when Hollis arrived for his, which would be much less suspicious than them turning up after him, then choosing a table nearby, or with a direct line of sight. They just had to take their chances—it was a delicate balancing act between getting the intel they needed, but without him noticing them too much. Obviously, as fellow guests of the hotel, it wasn't unusual that they should be there, but if he got even the slightest inkling that there was something off about them, then he could bolt, tip off his contact, or both.

Using her time productively while Baxter was showering, she got her outfit for the day ready, then checked all the equipment she might need, depending on how things went. As long as she was prepared for anything and everything, she'd be fine. *They'd* be fine.

Just as she'd packed her bag, her phone bleeped.

Hope you've got a fun day sightseeing planned. You might even make some friends—there are plenty of tourists in that area, from all over.

Mallory smiled and shook her head. Sometimes the coded messages she received were so innocuous that she could almost forget they *were* coded. Perhaps she really *was* on holiday with her boyfriend, having fun and taking in the local attractions. *If only.*

Quickly, though, the seriousness of the message's content sunk in. It actually meant that HQ had received some intelligence to indicate the Russian was heading to the area today. It made sense that the meeting would be today: Hollis wouldn't want to hang around too long in case the British government was onto him—he wasn't to know they already were—and the Russian would probably be in and out within the blink of an eye for similar reasons. Their window of opportunity was small, but she was certain they could pull it off. She had confidence in her own abilities, and Baxter was already showing great promise. She still had to keep an eye on him, of course, but she didn't feel like she had to watch him so closely that she might miss anything important. The vast majority of her attention could be aimed where it was supposed to be, with just a tiny bit to ensure Baxter was behaving appropriately.

She took in a deep breath, and released it. Then she hit reply and typed:

Sure have. Just getting cleaned up ready for breakfast—we'll need our energy for our busy day sightseeing and making friends! Will send some pics later on.

She sent the message.

The bathroom door clicked open. Mallory put her phone

down and pulled the robe more tightly around her body before turning in that direction.

Baxter strode out in nothing but a towel wrapped around his waist, a billow of steam following him. He smiled, a glint in his eye telling her that she wasn't the only one feeling fabulous after their night of passion. "Good morning."

"Morning!" she replied brightly, hurrying past him and towards the bathroom. She threw over her shoulder, "I'll be as quick as I can—we've had word that the Russian is coming to town today, so we need to get down to breakfast before Hollis does."

"Oka—" His response was cut off as she closed the bathroom door behind her.

A trickle of guilt seeped into her stomach, but she couldn't consider that right now. She couldn't consider *anything* that wasn't work-related. She needed to shower and dress, and she and Baxter needed to get down to the hotel restaurant as soon as possible.

Twenty minutes later, she and Baxter were heading for a table. They'd been greeted by a waitress who'd asked for their room number and had then told them they could sit wherever they liked. After a quick glance around had confirmed their target had not yet arrived, they hedged their bets by snagging a place right in the centre of the room—at least that way, wherever Hollis sat, he wouldn't be too far away from them. Mallory's specially modified phone had eavesdropping capabilities, so if he was out of human earshot, she could fire up the relevant app and let the technology do the work. Naturally that would only help if he spoke on the phone or in person to someone—it was useless if he was texting or emailing. But then, hopefully HQ were on the case in that regard and would forward on any useful information.

"Want to wait here while I get us a drink, so no one takes our table?" Baxter asked.

Mallory met his gaze and gave a warm smile. He really was very good for a beginner. "Great idea. I'll have tea, please."

"Coming right up." Baxter sauntered over to the buffet tables, where the breakfast food and drink was laid out. She watched him, hardly realising she was still smiling. When she did, she was going to stop herself until she remembered their cover—they were a couple in love, so gazing fondly at him with a silly grin on her face was perfectly natural. Even better, it meant she had an improved view of the door in her peripheral vision, so she clocked their target the exact moment he entered the room.

Appearing completely at ease, he headed straight for the buffet tables and ended up right beside Baxter. Mallory's heartbeat stuttered, but she forced herself to remain calm and fix her face in a relaxed, idle expression, so that anyone that might be paying her any attention wouldn't think anything of her looking at her boyfriend. They certainly wouldn't have any idea that she was carefully watching the body language of both men, as well as their lips to try to pick up what they were saying. As far as she could tell, they exchanged a "good morning", followed by Hollis commenting on what a nice day it was. Baxter responded politely in the affirmative. He said something else after that, but she wasn't sure what it was. She tried not to panic—after all, Hollis didn't react negatively to what Baxter had said. In fact, he smiled and nodded, then said something about a meeting. Thankfully, Baxter had by then finished making their drinks, so he extricated himself from the conversation with a parting, "Hope your meeting goes well," to which Hollis responded, "Thank you. Have a great day sightseeing."

It was all very innocent and meaningless, but she wished it had been her at that buffet table instead of Baxter. She might have been able to subtly extract more information from the man, or read more into his body language, his facial expression, his tone of voice. Anything that could give them a lead. But she couldn't change the past, and besides, Baxter had done well. He'd been put into an unexpected situation and had coped amazingly. He might not have found anything out, but at the same time he hadn't behaved oddly or suspiciously, either. She'd definitely class that as a win, a big tick in Baxter's suitability-to-join-the-team box.

She continued smiling benignly as Baxter returned to their table and put down their drinks. "Thanks, babe," she said, picking up the teaspoon from the saucer with one hand and reaching for the milk with the other. She added milk before handing the small jug to Baxter. "I'm so ready for this. I think I'm going to drink it first while I wake up a bit, then go and get something to eat." She fixed him with a meaningful look, hoping he'd take the hint that she was buying them some time so they could see what Hollis was going to do. If he only had a light breakfast of cereal or toast, then they would, too. If he was going for a cooked breakfast, then the same applied. Basically, they needed to time their exit from the restaurant as closely as possible with his without it being conspicuous. They could then figure out his next move—was he going straight to his meeting, or did he have time to kill first?

Baxter nodded. "That's fine, babe. There's no rush—we're on holiday, remember? Plus I imagine most of the tourist attractions won't open until nine or ten o'clock."

"True," she replied breezily, taking a sip of her drink while her brain buzzed madly, trying to figure out the best way to proceed. If Hollis headed straight out after breakfast, they'd have to find a way to keep an eye on him without being spotted. That would be much more difficult without crowds to hide in, or stores to pretend to browse in. She was fairly certain that, given his lack of transport, the meeting was taking place here in town—but where? Cafes, churches and museums were all popular locations for clandestine talks or exchanges of information, but other than following him, how could they know the chosen spot?

Damn it—no wonder I prefer big, crowded cities. It's so much easier to be anonymous.

In this case, adopting disguises probably wouldn't work—Hollis had, by now, got a very good look at Baxter, and a fairly good look at her. And unless by some stroke of luck coach loads of tourists came to the city today, they wouldn't have the option of disappearing into crowds. If he saw them and realised they'd attempted to mask their identities, he would bolt for sure. He might not be a fellow agent, or someone that was used to this kind of life, but nor was he an idiot. He wouldn't have gotten this far along with his dangerous plan if he was.

By the time she'd finished her cup of tea, the only solution that Mallory had come up with was one she really, really didn't like. She'd have to get HQ to mobilise someone else to tail their target for a while, just until they knew where and when the meeting was happening. Once that was established, if they could find a way to slip into the same place without standing out, they would. If not, they'd observe from a distance, utilising cameras and hi-tech listening devices. As soon as they'd gathered enough information to guarantee a conviction for both men, the team would be called in to make the arrests.

They were close now, so very close, and Mallory was determined to complete this mission without a hitch.

Chapter Twenty-Three

Several hours later, Mallory and Baxter were eating an impromptu picnic lunch on a park bench when they got the information they'd been waiting for. Hollis had finally left the hotel.

Mallory showed Baxter the text message.

"Thank God for that," he said, "my bum's going numb sitting here."

Mallory couldn't help but smirk. They *had* been sitting around for a while. After breakfast, Hollis had gone back up to his room, which at first hadn't presented a problem—they'd needed to go back up and brush their teeth and grab their bags for the day, in any case. But when he hadn't left again, they were left wondering what best to do. If they, too, stayed in their room, it would look incredibly dodgy—they were posing as tourists, after all. They wouldn't get much sightseeing done from the hotel. It'd be even worse if they left the building at the same time as their target—he knew for a fact they were supposed to be sightseeing, and to "coincidentally" bump into them yet again would be sure to set off some alarm bells.

After some deliberation, they'd decided their best bet was to head out into the city and kill time. They stayed fairly close to the hotel—within a couple of streets—so they could fall in quickly when needed. The killing time part was tough, though. It was dangerous to do anything too boring, because they might find themselves feeling sleepy, or losing focus. They needed their minds kept active, alert. So when ten minutes passed and their target still hadn't emerged, Mallory had suggested they *actually* do some sightseeing, but in places they could leave at the drop of a hat without attracting attention. A walk around the city centre, and visit to a church and a synagogue later, and their grumbling stomachs had sent them scurrying to a delicatessen, followed by the park bench, which they now vacated, after hurriedly clearing up their rubbish.

Just as they strode away from the bench, Mallory's phone bleeped again. She looked around to see if anyone was nearby as she fished it from her pocket, then read the message as they headed out of the park. "Finally—we have a location," she said. "Clever bastards. If the Russian didn't divulge the meeting place beforehand, there's no way anyone surveilling either of them could check it out or install any cameras or listening devices. And obviously if their meeting is imminent, there's no way we can get in there now. Right. The grab team is already on standby, so it's down to us now. We have to get eyes on that café, fast, then get ourselves somewhere that overlooks it. We've got all the kit we need to catch these fuckers red-handed, then send the boys in to pick them up."

She tapped out a coded reply that they were on their way, then smiled sweetly up at Baxter as she slipped her hand into his. "Come on, babe, let's go."

"Where are we going?"

They were out on the street now and there were a few people around, so she couldn't risk an open response. She squeezed his hand. "You'll see."

Their exploration of the city now came in handy—it meant she knew exactly where they were headed without having to consult a guidebook or Google Maps. That, and the increased pace at which they were walking, probably made them look much less touristy, but at this stage it was worth the risk. If they missed the whole exchange, or even part of it, and didn't get the evidence they needed, they could still grab both men, but they'd be relying more heavily on possible confessions and the possession of the stolen information, and whatever had been given to the Brit target in return for that information.

When British national security was at risk, a slight break in cover was excusable.

As they approached the end of the street which housed the meet point, Mallory slowed down. In spite of her racing heart, she felt calm. A calmness born of practice and confidence in her abilities. "Anything in your peripheral, Clark?" she asked quietly.

A couple of seconds later, he replied, "No."

"Good." She checked hers. Still in a low voice, she added, "Same. Looks like we beat Hollis here, in any case. But his friend could be anywhere—we don't know what he looks like. He could already be in the café, so don't pay any undue attention in that direction once we get there, all right?"

"Roger that."

They continued into the street at a much more leisurely pace. The café in question was around two-thirds down on the right hand side, which bought Mallory a little time to make a plan. She just hoped they'd get lucky with one of the properties on the opposite side of the street, which fortunately was pedestrianised, meaning there would be no vehicles blocking their view, and that anyone approaching would have to do so on foot.

As they drew closer, Mallory saw that they had, so far, got lucky. Across from the café was what looked to be a small hotel. She smiled—that was good news indeed. Another café would have been okay, or a shop, but any spying they did would be difficult to hide from the general public. In a hotel, all they had to do was find an empty room that provided them a decent view of the establishment opposite it, close and lock the door behind them and get down to the very important business of catching a traitor.

There was a downside, however. If Hollis was now in the area—and he certainly couldn't be too far behind them at this point—and saw them going into a hotel, he'd think it odd, since they already had a place to stay.

An idea occurred to her. "Hey!" She squeezed Baxter's hand again, not allowing her brain to linger on just how nice it was to hold hands with him in the first place. "Look at this—isn't it beautiful? Will you take my photo, sweetheart?"

The "it" she was talking about was the hotel building itself. She observed the tiniest flicker of confusion in Baxter's eyes, but then it was gone. He looked where she was pointing with her free hand, and nodded. "Yes, of course. It is stunning. Like you." He leaned down and gave her a quick kiss on the lips, before releasing her hand and stepping back while getting his phone out of his pocket.

Stopping her surprise in its tracks before it could manifest on her face, she pasted on a smile before backing up to the building and striking a pose. From this position, and with her sunglasses hiding her eyes, she could get a damn good look at the road, at anyone in the area, and into the café. The whole time she was faking what she hoped was a convincingly cute pose for one half of a couple on holiday, she was scanning faces, checking out potential exit points and peering into the establishment opposite.

"All done, babe," Baxter said, walking back over to her. "Here—what do you think?" He showed her the phone, which she made a big pretence of examining intently because, as she'd taken a second peek up and down the street, she'd spotted Hollis.

"Aww, that's great, baby. Thank you." She stretched up and gave him a kiss, which she allowed to linger. "Kiss me back," she murmured against his lips, hoping he could understand her muffled words.

      Baxter didn't hesitate. Immediately, his free arm went around her back and hauled her to him, while the arm holding the phone rested against her side. His mouth took hers so sensually, so passionately, that even she had trouble remembering that it was all for show. She was sure they were getting some sideways glances, and probably causing some nudges and giggles from people that passed them, but it was a necessary evil. It was clear Hollis would see them, engaging in a public display of affection as they were, but if they were "otherwise occupied", there was no way he'd approach them, and he wouldn't know that they'd seen him. As soon as he was safely ensconced in the café, they'd make a dash for the hotel.

      When an appropriate amount of time had passed, Mallory slowly broke the kiss, but kept her face close to Baxter's. She moved slightly to peer around his head at the café. *Bingo.* Their target was just pushing the door open. If he happened to turn and look at them again now, he'd think they were still playing tonsil tennis.

      Once the door had swung closed behind him, she waited another second to be sure he wouldn't turn, then grasped Baxter's arm and practically dragged him into the hotel. Who knew—if anyone else noticed their display, they'd perhaps think their kiss had caused her to be overwhelmed with passion for her lover, hence her leading him into the nearest hotel. If so, they'd laugh, shake their heads, and forget all about it.

      Baxter played along gamely, following her quickly as they entered the establishment. They had to find an empty room at the front of the building, on either the ground or first floors, and get in there quickly.

      A young woman, looking startled at their sudden and noisy arrival, stood behind the reception desk. Mallory made a snap decision. "Baxter, you have to take care of this. Either feed her some bullshit or stall her. As long as she doesn't interrupt me or call anyone."

      He nodded. "On it."

      She glanced around, and immediately spotted a door off to one side which had a sign saying *Staff Only.* As she ran towards it, she hoped like hell for two things: that it wasn't locked, and that the receptionist wasn't a lesbian.

      A moment later, as the door swung open, she had her first answer. The second would have to wait.

She'd entered some kind of office, which was mercifully empty. She wasn't altogether surprised—such a small establishment wouldn't need many staff. Even better, the room's small window afforded her a perfect view of the meet point. After locking the door behind her—there was, after all, a chance that Baxter's charms might fail—she jogged over to the window, removing her backpack as she went.

Mallory took the relevant equipment from the bag and got to work. After checking and double-checking that nobody outside was looking at her tiny window, she set up the specialist camera with its mega-zoom function and trained it on the café. She peered at the screen, then shifted the device and pressed buttons until she had Hollis right in the middle of the shot. For now, he was alone, which was perfectly fine with her. It bought her the time she needed to set up the directional microphone, which was much more powerful and hi-tech than the one built into her phone. But then, it was also much bigger and therefore no good for eavesdropping out in the open. In this situation, it was perfect.

Just as she'd gotten everything organised and recording, she saw a man enter the café. Could this be him? She watched on the screen as the tall, thin man walked right up to Hollis's table without hesitation and took a seat opposite him—which, by some miracle, provided the camera a perfect view of any interaction or transaction between the two men. The microphone even picked up the scrape of the chair legs on the tiled floor. That boded well for being able to listen in on and record the rest of the meeting.

"Hello," said a deep, heavily accented voice. "You came alone, yes? You were not followed?"

Hollis nodded, then quickly shook his head. "Yes. And no." He sounded breathless—he was clearly nervous. *He's shitting himself. Good. Serves him bloody right for betraying his country.* "I-I mean, yes I came alone, and no, I wasn't followed."

"Very good. You have made order for drinks?"

"Y-yes—oh, here it is now, actually."

That was a smart move on the Russian's part. He didn't want to hang around too long, but nor did he want to draw attention to them or piss off the management by sitting in a café and not purchasing anything, so he'd had Hollis pre-order. Even if neither of them touched the drinks, it would still look more natural than an empty table.

Both men leaned back in their chairs and smiled politely as the waitress arrived at the table. "Hello," she said in English, having already conversed with Hollis. She had no way of knowing his friend wasn't of the same nationality. "Two coffees. Would you like anything else?"

"No, thank you," Hollis replied. The Russian shook his head, but remained silent.

The girl nodded once, then picked up her tray and went back behind the counter.

As soon as the waitress was gone, the two men leaned forward again, ready to begin their business. The Russian spoke first. "So, you have the information for me?"

Mallory's mouth went dry. This was it—the exchange was happening. She already had her phone in her hand, her thumb hovering over the button which would send the message to mobilise the grab team. She itched to press it, to get these two bastards picked up and behind bars, but she had to wait, just a little longer.

"Yes," replied Hollis. He glanced around, then in a lower voice, continued, "Do you have the money?"

"Yes."

Neither man moved. *Come on, come on! Stop fucking posturing and get on with it.*

The Russian sighed. "Show me."

"You show me."

"I will squash you like bug and take it from you if you do not hurry. We should not linger here."

Mallory wasn't sure which part of the Russian's statement had spurred Hollis into action, but it didn't really matter. What mattered was him reaching into the inside pocket of his jacket and pulling out a memory stick. *Yes!*

"The money?" Hollis repeated.

The Russian sighed again, but reached into his own jacket pocket and retrieved a padded envelope. A *bulging* padded envelope. "This is show of good will. Once I have returned to my country, my computer people will make check of your information. If it is good, we will transfer rest of money into your account."

"And if you don't?" His hand curled tightly around the memory stick.

Waving the envelope, the Russian replied, "Then you will still be very rich man. But, like I say, if your information is good, you will get rest of money. I am not here to make games with you. If you do not trust me, you should leave now."

A tense moment followed in which Mallory felt the situation could go either way. But Hollis's greed won out—he was clearly willing to take the risk, even if it meant only having a portion of the money. Not that it mattered—he wouldn't get the opportunity to spend a penny of it. As his hand relaxed, and the Russian's in turn lowered the envelope towards the table, she gave the go signal to the grab team.

Got you, you fucking bastards.

Chapter Twenty-Four

Twenty-four hours later

Mallory paused for a moment outside Wesley's office, took a deep breath, then knocked on the door.

"Come in!"

Arranging her face into what she hoped was a neutral expression, she entered the room. "Hello, sir."

Her boss, seated behind his desk, gave a small smile. "Ah, Spider. Good to see you back. Please, sit down."

Mallory obeyed, then waited politely for Wesley to speak.

"So," he said, resting his elbows on the desk and steepling his fingers, a habit of his, "the operation was a success."

"It was, sir. Both our targets were captured, the intelligence and some money retrieved, and there is recorded evidence of the exchange, as well as eye witness reports."

"Very good. A job well done, particularly since it was a little out of your usual area of expertise, and at such short notice, with zero time for preparation."

She nodded. "Thank you. I'm just glad we got our men."

"Ye-es…" He bent his fingers now, and rested his chin on the flattened knuckles. "Speaking of *we*, how did Collinson get on?"

She'd been expecting this query, of course, so already had a reply prepared. "Very well indeed, sir. He followed instructions, but he also showed his own initiative, performed under pressure and maintained his cover. I would say, if I may, sir, that he shows great promise. I think he will make a very good agent."

Wesley looked thoughtful for a moment, then nodded. "I'm pleased to hear it. I'd much rather recruit a man than send him to jail. But tell me, are you singing Collinson's praises because he deserves it, or because of your relationship with him?"

Her heart raced, and she fought hard to keep the neutral expression on her face. She doubted she'd fool the old spymaster, but she had to at least try. "I have no relationship with him, sir, beyond that of colleagues." It wasn't a lie—the last day had been such a whirlwind of questioning, reporting, passing information and travelling that she and Baxter hadn't exchanged a word with each other that wasn't related to the mission. And, as far as she was concerned, an impromptu night together did not make them a couple, no matter what their actual feelings were on the matter.

"Hmm…" Wesley narrowed his eyes. "I know you wouldn't lie to me, Spider, so I'll rephrase that. Is it because of your feelings for him?"

Well, fuck. He had her there. She sighed and slumped back in the chair. Then, after a beat, indignation filled her and she straightened again. "Hey, wait just a minute! With all due respect, sir, you're right. I *wouldn't* lie to you, about anything. So I certainly wouldn't lie to you about something so important as the capability of a potential new recruit. No matter what my personal feelings were for someone—if it was my mother, my brother or Brad Pitt—I would give an honest appraisal of their abilities. There's no way I would risk the safety of myself, other agents, members of the public, or my country. It just wouldn't happen."

Wesley put his hands up, a smirk now on his lined face. "All right, all right. Calm down. Crikey—I've never seen you get so riled up. I'm sorry, I shouldn't have baited you like that—I just wanted to see how you would react. This, erm," he paused, thought for a moment, then continued, "*non-relationship* between yourself and Collinson has caused me a few sleepless nights, I don't mind telling you."

"Sir?" She frowned, her pulse still pounding and her stomach roiling. Just what was he getting at? It didn't seem like she was about to get a bollocking, so what was the point of this?

He sighed. "Okay—you've been honest with me, so it's time I was honest with you. I've been aware for a while that there's… something… between you and Collinson. I don't think for a moment you've acted on it—outside of what happened in Amsterdam, that is, but it's there nonetheless, bubbling away beneath the surface. My first reaction was to send Collinson somewhere else, away from here, away from you. But I stayed my hand because I couldn't help wondering whether it was something we could actually use to our benefit, terrible as that sounds.

"As you know, agents that can act as convincing couples are incredibly helpful in certain operations. Our people are the best in the world at what they do, but it doesn't change the fact that, if a target is paranoid, he or she will be much more focussed on looking for a single face on the street than a couple. And when it comes to infiltration-style tactics, criminals will be less wary of a young, good-looking couple than a lone woman."

He stopped for a moment, took a breath. Mallory nodded

slowly, still not quite grasping what Wesley's point was. She wasn't convinced he'd yet finished telling her the whole story. "So… you want Collinson and I to work together, posing as a couple?" She shrugged, though she wasn't quite as nonchalant about it as she was trying to convey. "I don't have a problem with that, sir."

Wesley pursed his lips and let out a heavy breath through his nostrils. "This is where things get murky, Spider. If it *was* just posing, then there would be no issue with it. But I'm worried that the more the pair of you fake it, the more your true feelings will get involved until it's not clear where the job ends and real life begins. Despite what you all may think of me, I *am* human, and I understand we're not emotionless machines, programmed to follow orders, do the job, rinse and repeat. In fact, in many cases, it's emotions, reactions, our very humanity that makes us so effective. To do the job well, we have to *care.* And I know you care, Spider, you care deeply. You're one of my top agents, and I want the best for you. But as you know, relationships with colleagues are deeply discouraged. The usual solution is to move one of the persons involved to another department.

"However, though that might be the 'by the book' way to do it, I'm not so sure it's the right solution here. Collinson is far from finished with his training, and as you say, he's been doing very well, and shows incredible potential. I don't want to throw that away on a bunch of what-ifs. So… what I propose is this: inside the office, so to speak, the pair of you continue as you have been. You worked very well together in Romania—despite being thrown in at the deep end, you passed that particular test with flying colours—and I think you'll continue to do so."

So it was a test.

"Outside of the office, however, is your business. Carry on with your non-relationship, or have it out and see where things go from there—whatever you want. But whatever you decide, you have to be absolutely sure that it's the right thing for everyone involved: the two of you, your colleagues and the country. The moment there's even the slightest whiff of an issue, you need to let me know. This could go either way—it could end up being the best partnership since Sherlock Holmes and John Watson, or it could end up with Collinson being transferred. Oh, don't worry," he added, spotting her horrified expression, "I'm not going to throw him in prison. As we've established, he's got potential, so even if he's not working in this department, we can find a use for him elsewhere. So please don't let that be a defining factor in your decision. And it is *your* decision—yours and Collinson's. It's unorthodox, I know. I may as well throw the rule book into the Thames. But I trust you to know what's best. All these years and you've never put a foot wrong. I don't think you're about to start now. Can I please stop talking? I'm getting a sore throat."

Mallory chuckled along with her boss, though at the moment, she was finding the situation far from amusing. If she had understood Wesley correctly, he was essentially saying that he—and God knows who else—knew there was a personal connection between her and Baxter, and that as long as it didn't impact their jobs in any way, they could act on that connection however they saw fit?

She was confused and flattered all at once. Confused that this was even a possibility, but flattered that Wesley had seen fit to bend—no, make that obliterate—the rules for her. Because he trusted her.

Would he be so understanding, so accommodating, if he knew that they had acted on their feelings? Multiple times, in a Brasov hotel room?

She pushed the thought to the back of her mind. It was no good looking a gift horse in the mouth. They—her and Baxter, that was—were being offered a golden opportunity. They *had* worked well together, and she was sure that could only improve as time went on. Unless something went sour in their private lives, that was. She couldn't guarantee they could behave professionally in the office if that happened.

But then, to echo her boss's sentiment—why throw it all away on a bunch of what-ifs? Her entire career was based on risk, and she'd done okay so far.

"Mallory? When I stopped talking, I expected you to have something to say."

She snapped her attention back to her boss. "Oh, sorry, sir. It's just a lot to take in. I'm struggling to get my head around it all. It's very unexpected."

Wesley gave a wry smile. "I would have thought in our line of work, you'd have learned to expect the unexpected."

Now her chuckle was heartfelt. "I have, sir. But this isn't work—this is different."

"True. So, are you going to tell Collinson, or am I?"

Letting her innermost feelings show in front of her boss for the first time ever, Mallory grinned a Cheshire cat grin. Her heart pounded again, but this time it was with excitement and anticipation. "If it's all the same to you, sir, I think I'd like to have the privilege."

Wesley gave a nod. "Fair enough. So, unless there's anything else you need to report, you're dismissed." He looked at his watch, then back at Mallory. "I believe he's in the gymnasium. You have one hour, and then I expect you both to be back to work. Understand?"

Jumping to her feet, Mallory nodded. "Yes! Yes, sir!" Her mind still whirling with questions and possibilities, she could hardly decide what to do next. Part of her wanted to rush around the desk and kiss Wesley, but that would just be bizarre.

No, if she was giving out kisses, there was someone much more appropriate to receive one. And apparently, he was in the gymnasium.

With a final "thank you" flung in her boss's direction, she hurried from the room. They only had an hour, after all. And then possibly, just possibly, the rest of their lives.

About the Author

Lucy Felthouse is the award-winning author of erotic romance novels *Stately Pleasures* (named in the top 5 of Cliterati.co.uk's 100 Modern Erotic Classics That You've Never Heard Of, and an Amazon bestseller), *Eyes Wide Open* (winner of the Love Romances Café's Best Ménage Book 2015 award, and an Amazon bestseller) and *The Persecution of the Wolves*. Including novels, short stories and novellas, she has over 160 publications to her name. She owns Erotica For All, and is one eighth of The Brit Babes.

Web and social media links:
Website: http://www.lucyfelthouse.co.uk
Twitter: http://www.twitter.com/cw1985
Facebook: http://www.facebook.com/lucyfelthousewriter
Newsletter: http://www.subscribepage.com/lfnewsletter
Amazon: http://author.to/lucyfelthouse
BookBub: https://www.bookbub.com/authors/lucy-felthouse

If You Enjoyed Hiding in Plain Sight

If you enjoyed *Hiding in Plain Sight*, you may also enjoy my other M/F books. Visit my website (http://lucyfelthouse.co.uk) to find out more about these titles, and to see my full list of books.

City Nights: One Night in Paris
Jacob is nearly forty, and has recently come to the sudden realisation that he's not doing much with his life. Sure, he's got his own successful business, but what's the point in earning lots of money and not doing anything or going anywhere to spend it?

He's in serious danger of being all work and no play, so he starts to rectify this by organising a twenty four hour layover in Paris en route to a meeting in Dubai. Whilst there, he goes on a bus tour of the city, and there meets Annabelle, a fellow Brit who's studying in Paris. There's clearly an attraction between the two of them, so when the gorgeous Annabelle makes an indecent proposal to help Jacob fill his time in Paris, who is he to refuse?

City Nights: One Night in Budapest
Hermione's in Budapest on a romantic weekend break. Or at least it should have been romantic—an unexpected break-up means she's visiting the Hungarian capital alone. Determined to make the most of it, she goes on a night-time river cruise, the perfect opportunity to see some of the city's beautiful sights after dark.

On the boat, cute Budapest native Emil serves her cocktails. They chat a little on the journey, engage in some banter, and when Emil asks Hermione out for dinner, she's seriously tempted. But she's a long way from home, by herself—is dinner with a complete stranger a good idea? Hermione decides to take a chance, and what follows is an unforgettable night which will transform her life forever.

Mean Girls
Adele Blackthorne is a big girl, a curvy chick. She knows it, and she's been picked on all her life because of it. But she's gotten to the stage where she doesn't care. She may be Rubenesque, but she's healthy, too. Much healthier than the mean girls at the leisure

center that point and stare and say spiteful things about her. Adele rises above it all, and simply enjoys her secretive glances at the center's hunky lifeguard, Oliver.

As the bullying of Adele becomes worse, Oliver finds it increasingly difficult not to intervene. He doesn't want to get into trouble with work, but equally he can't stand to see Adele treated in such a horrible way. Especially since he doesn't agree that she's fat and unattractive. He thinks she's a seriously sexy woman, and would like to get to know her better. Much better.

Printed in Great Britain
by Amazon